★   ★   ★

young americans

★   ★

For my brother

young americans

jeff gomez

SCHOLASTIC
PRESS

Scholastic Children's Books,
Commonwealth House, 1–19 New Oxford Street,
London WC1A 1NU, UK
a division of Scholastic Ltd
London ~ New York ~ Toronto ~ Sydney ~ Auckland
Mexico City ~ New Delhi ~ Hong Kong

Published in the UK by Scholastic Ltd, 2000

Text copyright © Jeff Gomez, 2000

ISBN 0 439 01292 9

Typeset by M Rules
Printed by Cox and Wyman Ltd, Reading, Berks.

2 4 6 8 10 9 7 5 3 1

*"I know of no greater gift than to be young,
and of no greater fear than to lose one's youth;
it is the one thing of value which we are all given.
Pity that it must be spent, and cannot be saved."*

*– Alec Walther
1781–1836*

Let me begin this story by telling you that I come from a broken home. In fact, I wouldn't even call it broken; it's worse than broken. I come from a home with multiple fractures.

My parents divorced when I was pretty young. I was maybe two or three at the time; I don't even know for sure exactly how old I was because I wasn't in school yet, so I didn't have the sense to look at a calendar and mark down a date. In fact, when it all happened I didn't know what a calendar was. I might not even have been walking or talking at the time. I might've been *that* young. All I remember is, suddenly, there was a lot more space in the house. After that final slam of the front door when my dad left, none of the other doors were ever slammed again. Whatever excuse my mom gave for his absence is lost on me; I can't remember a thing about it except that, pretty quickly, I swallowed the fact and learned to live without him.

I have an older brother, and I guess for a time he took my father's place, the way pretty much anyone who was male and bigger than I was easily would have. Josh is twice my age – nearly thirty by now, he lives in Manhattan and just got married – and, until he left for college, he was a pretty good surrogate dad: making dinner, helping me with my homework, picking me up from soccer practice and picking me up from the dirt after getting hit in the head by too many soccer balls during practice. I don't see him much these days – ever since he graduated he's visited maybe once a year, usually at Christmas, which is when even the most distant of families tend to gravitate towards each other – but whenever we talk on the phone and we laugh and tell jokes or remember the good times we spent when I was growing up and he was almost already there, I can still hear in his voice that singular sort of understanding that makes me believe that no one will ever know me like he does.

After Josh left is when Mom and I began to move around. The first summer after he was gone, she met Ron, which led to her second divorce, which somehow seemed to pave the way for her third and fourth. For the next couple of years she drifted from marriage to marriage, and in between the towns we tried to settle in (though we never stayed long, each of our New Lives were like glue which refused to really harden), we rotated from relative to relative, living for brief periods in various towns and states all over the country. Spread across America I've got three sets of step-parents, four half-brothers, five half-sisters, six grandparents (only two of which are real), and too many cousins and aunts and uncles to count. Most people look at a map and all they see are roads and highways, but I look at a map like it's my family tree.

Our new home this time is in Walther, which is a little town in New York State I've never been to or even seen a picture of. Once again I'm finding myself miles away from everything I knew, or at least everything I had gotten to know in the past eleven months since it was the last time we moved.

When I was young I guess I didn't mind all this too much because it seemed like an adventure, and I actually used to feel sorry for kids who have had to live their whole lives in just one town, with just one house and just one set of friends. Wherever Mom and I went, it was always sort of fun to start all over again – new school, new friends. Something new is usually exciting. But now, the older I get (I'll be fifteen next February), moving around isn't so much fun. In fact, it's a drag. I'm getting tired of always having to start over, of always being the outsider at school, of never knowing my way around town.

I know that a lot of this probably sounds sad or tragic, and maybe it is, but I swear I'm not trying to elicit sympathy or coax out tears or anything. When I was a kid, maybe that would have been the goal, like the way you try and convince a parent to let you stay home from school by acting sick when you're really not. But I don't do that any more – try to push people into believing anything about me – and that's not what I'm trying to do now. I'm just trying to be honest, and if it's coming out a frown instead of the other way round, there's nothing I can do about all that because what's done is done and I can't worry about the past, I can only work on the future. I can only worry about this summer, and the fact that Mom and I have moved to a new town and that I've got only three months to make new friends before the school year starts – my first year of high school.

For everyone else in Walther, this is going to be just another summer. But for me it's going to be like running a race, with my new life sitting just across the finish line.

june

"For God's sake, Perry, won't you give Sis a hand?"

My mother finds me hiding in what is going to be my room, if you can call it a room. It's really a converted linen closet off the main hallway of a blue and white two-story house that was built "before the war", but I'm afraid to ask *which* war. The house belongs to Mom's sister, who is named Sis (which is short for Sissy, even though I always thought *Sis* was just a sibling nickname, like when I call Josh *Bro*). We can't afford a house of our own – not yet – that's why, for now, we're sharing this one.

As boring as the rest of the house is, my room's not so bad. I've really got to hand it to Sis's boyfriend, Bob, who knocked out the wall of one of the kitchen's pantries, then took out the shelves and a thick wooden rod where coats used to hang in the closet, and shoved into the oddly shaped rectangle a twin-bed, dresser and even a desk. After a coat of paint, a lock on the inside (that was my idea), and a large Japanese-looking round paper lamp Mom bought at Pier One, it was ready to be lived in. As a room, it's not half bad. If I were grading this as one of Bob's projects (the way he grades his students all day; he teaches woodshop at Walther High), I'd give him a B, maybe even a B+.

"What?" I call back, even though I heard my mother perfectly the first time. In fact, her words are still ringing in my ears; chores always do. I ask her to repeat herself just to buy some time.

"I said, Periwinkle Mathews, that you ought to give Sis a hand. After all, half the things she's bringing in from the truck are *yours*."

Warily rising from the bed which Bob has wedged underneath where the roof slopes because of the staircase, I join my mom in the hall. I can see that Sis is carrying two boxes, both of which are marked TUPPERWARE. I know the boxes aren't heavy (it's just a bunch of cheap plastic containers for holding sandwiches and leftover casseroles), but Sis is straining and making faces as if she were trying to bench press three times her own weight. Sis is an awfully good actor.

"My name's *not* Periwinkle," I call back to my mom as she heads out to the U-Haul for yet another load. It's half-past five and we're almost done. I've never had to move with the help of only two females before, but I think if I had the choice to do it again, I'd rather do it alone. "My name's Penrod, and you know it."

I don't even know why we always have this argument; like Penrod's any better than Periwinkle?

"Your father chose *that* one. I chose Josh, your brother's name. Nice simple name."

She's right: there's nothing you can do with a name like *Josh*. No nickname, nothing.

"You," she points at me, "*Pen*rod. I don't know *how* I ever let him talk me into it."

The official story of why I was named Penrod, which really is, legally, my name, is that there is a fictional character my father loves who is also named Penrod. The character is a scrappy sort of kid, a lot like Tom Sawyer or Huckleberry Finn, and he was real popular about a hundred years ago. The writer's last name who created Penrod is Tarkington, but I always forget the man's first name, which is something unusual and starts with a B. The word "Booth" floats to my mind, but who would name their child that? But then again, who would name their child Penrod? My dad, who loves books and read three and four a day when he was my age, says that Tarkington's *Penrod* stories were the favourites of his youth; he liked them even better than anything by Mark Twain. (Thank God for that. I might have been named Huckleberry.) He decided way back then, when he was still just a kid, that one day, if he had a boy, the child would be named after his old hero. My mom didn't let him name their firstborn Penrod – she insisted against it – but by the time I came along she was worn out by motherhood from the first go round with Josh, and would have been open to anything. My brother was even born in a strange Russian way, underwater with my mom in a big tank like a small swimming-pool. I've heard that Josh was only the fourth baby to be born that way in the United States. But by the time I came along, eleven years later, my mother and father were bored with their old hippy ways, and I was delivered in a hospital just like every other kid. Instead of going through the pure and spiritual act of natural childbirth when I was born, my mother was pumped full of drugs and, she told me many years later, didn't feel a thing.

I've never much minded my name because everyone just calls me Perry. Whenever I meet a new kid or even an adult, and they ask who I am, "Perry" is what I always say. I'm glad no one knows I'm really named Penrod; it'd probably mean no end of trouble for me at school if they did.

Last year, in my math class, I met a kid named Jazz. He really was named Jazz. He even brought his birth certificate to school one day to prove it. Some of the other kids thought it was cool to have a name like that, to be so different. But I just felt sorry for him. Can you imagine trying to live up to a name like Jazz?

"Whatever your name is," my mom laughs, "will you just give Sis a hand? There's only two more boxes, and then we're through."

"Yeah, yeah," I grumble and head out the front of the house to where the orange and white van is parked half on the kerb, half sticking out in the street.

On the side of the van there's a brightly painted mural of the Statue of Liberty, the Empire State Building and the Brooklyn Bridge. Underneath this picture are the words NEW YORK, and next to this it says AMERICA'S MOVING ADVENTURE.

The painting reminds me of Josh, because he lives in Manhattan. I'm hoping that sometime this summer I can go and see him – him and his new wife, Kendra. They'd been dating for years and finally got married last March, but Mom and I have never met her. They were married at Kendra's parents' house in Ohio and, at the time, my mom and I were still living in Tucson with her *husband du jour*, and we didn't have the cash to fly and actually witness the wedding. My mom begged them to wait a while, to give her some time to save up the cash for the trip, but Josh was insistent on getting married right away. We all thought Kendra was pregnant, but it turns out she's not, so they must have been rushing things for some other reason.

The wedding pictures duly arrived a month afterwards. They were just snapshots, really: my brother in a dark blue suit with his arm around a blonde in a bone-white dress, along with various photos of strangers – who must have been Kendra's family – eating cake and dancing. There was one photo of Kendra alone, sitting on a bench underneath an awning with a glass of champagne in her hand and a smile on her face, that I stole from the pile of others. She's really attractive in that picture and whenever I look at it, I have to tell myself that this is just some girl from a magazine, like a model or something, because otherwise it's too creepy to have those kinds of thoughts about my brother's wife. After all, he gets to really sleep with her, but all I can do is stare. Maybe *creepy* is not how I really feel; maybe I'm just jealous.

My mom has been promising me that I'll be able to take a trip soon, that I don't have to stay in Walther for the entire summer. She keeps promising me a vacation, that maybe she'll send me to Manhattan, to see Josh and Kendra for a while. She keeps mentioning this like it's a reward for being so quiet and willing over the last couple of weeks. "Most kids would have kicked and screamed, having to pick up and move like that without any notice," she told me on the drive out here. When she said this, in my head I was thinking, *Most kids would have done worse than that.*

That's one of the reasons I didn't mind moving back to the East Coast, so I could be closer to Josh, so I might actually see my brother besides the one week a year at Christmas when he flies to wherever it is we're living.

Don't get me wrong. It's not that I was incredibly happy back in Tucson, and was all reluctant to leave, because I wasn't. The summers there were way too hot, the land was flat and dry (not like the full, green forests of the Pacific Northwest, which is where I'd been living for the three years before Arizona), and my stepdad (a man I had maybe eight conversations with in a year) was not really evil, but in a way he was worse than that:

he was boring. And yet life wasn't so bad. I had made some friends; as a kid, you have to. There was Scott and Tim and Ray and maybe two other guys with whom I could have lunch if Scott or Tim or Ray were out sick that day or else temporarily mad at me. Someone to have lunch with is very important. There's not too many things worse in the world than having to, day after day, eat your lunch alone. I learned this when I had to eat my meals isolated in the corner of the cafeteria – facing just a wall – for six months until I met Scott, who then introduced me to Tim. Ray was a friend of both of theirs. Before I met Scott in my English class I had stopped eating lunch altogether, and took to spending the way-too-long break in the library, pretending to read, pretending that I enjoyed being there.

I retrieve the last two boxes from where they've been piled in the very rear of the van, stuck behind the truck's wheel-wells so they wouldn't slide around, and cushioned with three blankets that smell like dust. I set them down first on the kerb before taking them into the house because, now that the van's empty, I need to close and lock the large sliding rear door. I think this is sort of ridiculous, to worry about somebody stealing something when there's nothing else in there, but Mom was worried someone might steal either the blankets or the refrigerator dolly which we didn't even end up using.

It takes all of my weight to close the folding metal door, and for a second I just dangle there, hanging on to the leather strap before the thing gives way, which makes a sound like an avalanche when it finally does. *Ker-rash!* When she hears the noise, my mom comes running out of Sis's house and shoots me a dirty look, as if I've woken up the entire neighbourhood, but that's impossible because the sun has hours to go before it sets.

As I slowly make my way up the red brick sidewalk, heading into the house – my new home – I turn around and take a last look at the moving van which Bob is coming by later to pick up. For some reason, the words AMERICA'S MOVING ADVENTURE catch my eye. Once inside the house I drop off the two boxes in the kitchen and then head to my room, the two converted closets which smells sourly of still-drying paint, and I think to myself, *Some adventure.*

When I wake up the next day, sometime around eleven, I feel lost. Worse than lost, I feel shipwrecked. I call out for Mom, for Sis, for anybody, but there's no one there. Then I realize it's Monday morning. They've both gone to work, my mother to her latest job as a realtor and Sis to an office where she does, nine hours a day, boring office type things: filing, typing, answering the phone, etc.

I turn my head and face a plastic alarm clock that's so old it still has hands instead of a digital face. The clock is one of the touches Bob added in order to make this closet feel more like a room.

I sit up in bed and, for a few seconds, can't remember

where I am. The past week has been a blur of dreary motel rooms; each one different, but somehow the same. Before that, I remember the last day of the eighth grade back in Arizona, saying goodbye to all of my friends. The next day I packed and stuffed all of my things into box after box, my mom sealing them all with brown tape while she yelled at me to hurry up.

Near the door of this dark bedroom – dark because there's no windows and I have no idea where to find the light switch – I see all of those boxes. There are four of them, each one marked PERRY'S THINGS.

Stumbling into the kitchen I find some milk and orange juice in the fridge and even a brand of cereal I like, which Sis must have bought especially for me since I doubt that she's a big fan of Fruit Loops. All of this makes me smile: the room that Bob built, these groceries which Sis picked up, and the note I find on the kitchen table: *Son, try to get out of the house today and see the town. Make some friends. I know you will. Together we can do this.*

After breakfast I decide to do as Mom says and check out the town. Besides, I feel a little creepy hanging around the house all by myself. I haven't even gone upstairs yet, because all that's upstairs is Sis's room and the spare bedroom which is now my mom's. In between there's a bathroom, but there's a bathroom downstairs, too, and that's the one I plan on using. Nothing's worse than having to use a bathroom shared by two women: all those strange bottles, all those weird smells. Brushing my teeth next to four pairs of black stockings might be sort of sexy, if only the stockings didn't belong to my mother and aunt.

Even though it's not even noon, it's already really hot outside. But this is a different kind of heat than what I'm used to. The air feels wet, sticky. The sky is slightly overcast and dark. In Portland, a day like today would have meant a cool breeze and refreshing rain, but on the East Coast – even though it's not bright and sunny – it's still hot. In Arizona it was a dry heat – sometimes I felt like an ant under a magnifying glass – but right now I'd prefer that to this hazy humid hell.

Getting to the main part of town turns out to be about a half-hour walk from Sis's house. Walther seems like a pretty small town, and at dinner last night (Pizza Hut, just like we used to get back in Tucson; when I closed my eyes and chewed I felt like I was still back there) Sis told us that Walther doesn't even have its own newspaper. Walther and two other towns join together to put out the *Tri-Countier*, which still isn't large enough to put out an issue every day. On Saturday there's no paper, but as if to make up for this the Sunday edition is twice as large.

Right in the centre of downtown is a large square park, at the end of which is an old building which at first I think is a museum, but turns out to be a library. Inside the park are dozens of iron benches, a few water fountains, a couple of gardens, and at the centre there's a large statue of a guy made out of metal standing at a podium or something like that. Underneath the white streaks left by the pigeons, the statue's sort of a pale green. I don't recognize who the statue is supposed to be, so I just keep on walking, through the square and on to the other side where a line of shops stand behind angled parking spaces, cars pointing forward with their trunks sticking out into the street.

On the corner there's a doctor's office. Then I pass a little bakery which smells like cookies; in fact, I pass it twice, sniffing like crazy each time. Then there's a little stationery store, then a drugstore, a pet shop and, on the other corner, a comic book store.

I go into the comic book store and sort of browse around, even though I've never really liked comics and don't even know where to begin. An old friend of mine from Tucson, Adam, really loved comics, the X-Men especially, so I guess I must have read one or two issues in my life. Personally, I always thought comics were a little immature, what with all the grown men dressed up and running around in tights and silly costumes. But Adam really liked them, so I acted as if I liked them, too. Sometimes it's amazing what you'll do for a friend.

But what I really can't believe is that this store – Ralph's Comic Kingdom, it's called – is filled not only with kids but also with adults. The grown-ups are right alongside the teenagers, grabbing at Batman and Superman, etc. I can even see that in the corner there's an X-rated section. X-rated comics? Goddamn, it'd have to be a pretty sexy drawing in order to get me as excited as a photograph of a woman with no clothes on.

Photographs may not be real, but at least there's some truth in them; they're pictures of something real, that really does exist. What I find so sexy about a photograph is that you know that that girl's out there somewhere, and the fantasy is that maybe one day you'll find her and she'll be all yours. But a drawing? You can't have sex with a drawing.

After a couple of minutes of just walking around in circles, I decide to go outside for some additional exploring. After all, it's early and I don't want to go home just yet. Neither Mom nor Sis will be back for hours, and I don't want to be in that old house alone any longer than I have to.

Down a side street which leads away from the gigantic library and town square, I can see a small park with a few basketball courts which are attached to an elementary school. Even from this distance, a block away, I can tell that the kids playing basketball are too old for elementary school, but I figure that since it's summer, every group of kids can run all over the other kids' schools. I remember doing that back in Portland, when I first started junior high. A few friends and me would go to this elementary school to play basketball because they still had the really small nets (and drinking fountains no higher than your knee). At our school they'd already set us up with regulation courts, as if we'd hit puberty since the sixth grade and all of us were as tall as Michael Jordan. The training wheels were off and we didn't like it. So we went back to our old school, pushed the little kids out of our way, and made slam-dunks and every free-throw shot until it got dark and we couldn't see the ball.

I start to walk down the street, towards the basketball game. I can see there's a lot of kids stuffed within the court which is surrounded by a rusted chain-link fence which has turned, over the years, from silver to brown. There's so many kids that not all of them can play at once. Almost a dozen skirt the sidelines, waiting for their chance; half have shirts on, the others don't. This causes me to immediately groan: shirts and skins. *Oh, Jesus, not that. Whose stupid idea was shirts and skins, anyway?*

Knowing I'll never have the nerve to actually try to play in the game, not if I have to take my shirt off (my chest is flabby and my skin is so white in areas I'm pink), I just walk up to the fence and watch. I think that maybe some other kid will see me watching, not recognize me, and strike up a conversation. After all, I've got a lot in common with a kid who isn't playing: neither of us is in the game.

After twenty or so points have been scored for both teams (which takes place in a matter of minutes; those five-foot-high nets really aren't much of a challenge), I notice that my presence is producing a hell of a lot of stares, but none of them are friendly. In fact, one kid looks at me, taps his friend on the shoulder and then points towards where I'm standing. Now they're both looking at me. Then, all of a sudden, the second guy who hadn't even noticed me in the first place taps yet another kid on the shoulder and points in my direction. I watch as this continues until the only ones with their eyes not on me are the players on the court, whose eyes are thankfully on the ball.

Without needing to be told, I quietly retreat from the court, slinking back towards the library. I figure I've seen these guys enough for now; besides, I'll probably be seeing a lot of them next year at school. Suddenly this thought burns me, makes me hotter than the heat ever could. I think that all of those guys are going to remember me, and they'll remember how I was snubbed, and because of that I'll never be able to get in good with any of them. Here I thought I'd be getting this fresh start and already I'm being left behind.

All of these thoughts make me really mad at my mom. She thought all of this was going to be so easy. She thinks that everyone under the age of sixteen is in some sort of club and that we all like and recognize each other based on a secret handshake or something, but that's just not true.

In the movies or on TV, whenever a kid moves to a new town, all he has to do to become popular is walk out of the house. Once outside, *Bang!*, he's got a whole group of friends, including a best friend and sometimes even a date. Sometimes all of this happens on the first day he arrives, usually at the beach or else a picnic or barbecue he somehow was miraculously invited to, all of his new friends saying, *Come on, join the fun, it won't be a party without you!* Yeah, right. Like all I have to do is snap my fingers and, *Presto!*, I'm Mr Popularity.

My mom must have seen those films and TV shows because she's never once hesitated picking up everything and moving us yet again to yet another town. She doesn't know that in real life things just aren't that easy. It's hard to make friends. Kids don't want to meet new kids, not unless they absolutely have to. When you're three or four or even five years old, it's different; anybody with a toy that you don't have is potentially your best friend. But if adults didn't keep sticking teenagers into different classes every year, I bet they'd never talk to someone other than their own group of friends. There'd be no reason to. Of course, when puberty hits and sex is suddenly involved, it's a totally different story. There are no such things as rules between boys and girls when hormones kick in. But if you're just talking about boys at my age, forget it. We're just not trained to be social. We can't make conversation and we don't want to.

After about ten minutes of walking around and around the square, I head down the row of shops on the opposite side of the park from where I went before. This time I pass a dry-cleaner, a video rental store, an ice-cream and frozen yogurt place, a tiny little post office and, on the corner, there's a diner.

With nothing else to do, I go inside. I'm not really hungry, but I know that, at the very least, the place will be air-conditioned and, with the heat outside and my anger inside, I feel like I'm about to burst. I need to cool off and calm down.

The diner is set up like one big hallway, with a counter running down the length of the room and a few tables in between an aisle, on the other side of which are five booths which look out on to the hot day. The floor is made up of black and white tiles, and all the chairs are upholstered in bright orange vinyl with shiny steel legs. Either this place was built in the fifties, or else someone has spent an awful lot of money to make it seem like it was. I look for a jukebox but can't find one, even though rockabilly music is coming from somewhere.

Not wanting to look like I'm a complete outcast, I take a seat at the counter, which is always better than sitting in a booth alone. Sitting in a booth all by yourself is death because when there's that much empty space, people can't help but feel sorry for you.

I hear a voice say, "What can I get for you?" even though I don't immediately look up to see whom it belongs to. It belongs to a waitress, obviously, but my eyes are trained on the laminated menu which says GUS'S DINER, and beneath this in script, *Making Food the Walther Way for Twenty-Five Years*. The menu is made up mostly of the usual things: burgers, sand-wiches, breakfast served all day.

"I'll have a cheeseburger," I say, to satisfy my stomach. In order to quench my thirst, I add ". . .and a large Sprite, please."

Finally I look up and see a young girl wearing clunky

white shoes and a yellow dress. Her strawberry-blonde hair is in a ponytail, and this exposes small ears pierced with a pair of baby-blue earrings. Her name tag says HI MY NAME IS DONNA and, for a few seconds, I'm paralyzed because she's so completely beautiful. It's not fair that she's taking my order. *I* should be waiting on *her*.

"Cheeseburger and a large Sprite, right?" She says this with her eyes closed, as if she were trying to memorize my order even though she's already written it down.

"Y-y-yes," I barely manage to get out.

My heart starts to beat fast and my face feels flushed and hot again, even though the inside of the diner is so air-conditioned it's almost *too* cold.

When she leaves to get my drink, I finally begin to calm down, and by the time she returns, I'm almost back to normal. In fact, I'm feeling sort of cocky and confident, so I decide to push my luck and make conversation. But for some stupid reason, the first thing I say is, "Did you just start working here?"

She quickly places my glass on the counter and then leans in and begins to speak in a whisper instead of the loud waitressy voice she greeted me with.

"Is it that obvious?"

Her face looks cracked in half with disappointment. It was a dumb thing to say, I know, but the only reason I asked was because she looked so young – she might even be my age – it wasn't because she was doing a lousy job or anything. Luckily, a little lie shoots right to the top of my head and there's no time to stop it before it spurts right out of my mouth.

"No, no, it's not obvious at all. I only suspected that you're new because you're so much nicer than a usual waitress. Normally they're old and mean. Missing teeth. Cranky. You know."

I can tell I said the right thing because her face lights up like a sunrise, while her whole body seems to grow inside her canary-coloured waitress uniform.

"Actually, I did just start. Well, not *just*. I started when school got out last week – but it's only a summer job. My parents want me to start saving for college. Can you believe it? It's a bit of a drag, I know, but they promise me I'll be able to spend some of the money on a car since I'll be getting my learner's permit *real* soon."

"You mean you're. . ." The word gets caught in my throat, "Fifteen?"

"Yeah, aren't you?"

For a few seconds I'm too stunned to answer. If a hole opens up beneath the bar stool I'm sitting on, I'll gladly jump in.

"No," I finally say, but only because sitting there silent looks stupid. "I'm just fourteen. But I'll be fifteen soon. Well, *next* year, that is."

"So you're, what, a *fresh*man?"

"Will be, yeah." Now the words are barely crawling their way out of my mouth. If the diner had any more customers, she wouldn't be able to hear my whispers. "And you?"

"Oh, uh, I'll be a sophomore . . . but it's no big deal. You know . . . uh . . . you'll *like* being a freshman. It's not *too* bad. Don't worry about what anybody says. I mean, there's nothing *wrong* with it. I mean, we *all* have to do it, right?"

At the counter behind her a bell is rung and a plate of food is shoved through a small window which connects the counter area with the kitchen behind it. Through the small slit I can see a large man standing over the grill with a cigarette in his mouth, a trail of ash dangling from the lit tip.

Donna, suddenly remembering that she's a waitress, jumps from where she's been leaning on the counter trying to console me, and grabs the plate from the steel ledge. She checks the ticket, then smiles wide. It's my cheeseburger.

"Here you go," she says cheerfully.

While setting down the burger in front of me, she watches as an older couple enters and sits down in a booth near the window which is part of her station. She must have the counter and half the booths to worry about. That seems like an awful lot for someone who just started.

After a few minutes of just picking at the burger and eating most of the fries (seeing the cook with that cigarette sort of killed my appetite), Donna comes over to check on me. I assure her everything's fine, that I'm just taking my time, don't want to rush it, etc.

We have a couple of nice little conversations in

between her filling up glasses with Coke or tea or coffee, and I realize that she really doesn't mind that I'm just going to be a freshman while she'll be a sophomore. I realize that the only one who has a problem with that fact is me. Here I was worrying she would judge me by my age or what grade I'm in, but she's not doing any of that. If anything I'm judging her, thinking she won't like me because I'm a little younger than she is and not even in high school yet. I tell myself to relax, to not worry so much and to stop thinking so fast and just enjoy this.

After an hour passes, and I discover I can't pick at this bun and meat and cheese any longer, I ask Donna for the check. She drops it with a smile and I leave her a big tip.

I get up to leave even though I'd like to stay to talk to her and maybe even do something crazy like ask her out on a date, but by now it's almost five and people are getting off work and coming into the diner for an early dinner.

Trying to get her attention I wave goodbye as I pass through the door, but it doesn't work. She doesn't see me. So I hide behind a cigarette machine and watch her, staring as she circles through the diner dropping off the various plates of food. I keep watching until someone puts three dollars in the vending machine but gets pissed off because it won't spit out his Camels, and I'm afraid Donna will see me as the guy starts kicking the cigarette machine and shouting out

"Goddamnit", over and over again. This is my cue, I figure, to leave.

At the end of three days of wandering around town, Mom refuses to believe that I haven't made a whole boatload of lifelong friends, so I lie to her. I don't feel good about lying, but I don't feel good about telling her how awful I am at making new friends, either. If she'd only try and understand. If she could, just for once, see the way things really are.

"So, tell me. . ."

It's Sis and Mom and me sitting around the large plastic table in the kitchen. I've been here almost a week now and we've yet to eat in the dining-room once. I wonder what kind of event it will take before I get to sit in one of those dark wooden chairs with the high back and the ornately carved arms. I'll probably have to wait until Thanksgiving or maybe Christmas. That's one of the funny things about adults – they have all this great stuff, but usually never use it.

What we're eating is fried chicken from a red and white striped bucket, along with coleslaw, biscuits and little containers of mashed potatoes buried beneath dollops of watery gravy. Mom picked it up on the way home from a fast-food place, using the drive-thru like she loves to do. As I helped her set the table, she told me she'd developed a craving for it sometime around midday – she didn't know why – and that she would have just died if we would've had anything other than fried chicken for dinner tonight. Mom gets them pretty bad sometimes – cravings. When she does, you'd better just get out of her way and let her satisfy whatever need she thinks she has; when she gets like that, it's like she's possessed.

"What do you want me to tell you?" I say, trying to peel the skin off my drumstick. The best thing about fried chicken is always the skin. They should just sell buckets of fried batter and nothing else. If they did, I'd eat it every day.

"Tell me about your new friends. Tell me about all the kids you've met."

There's silence for a few seconds before I answer, and looking across the table I can see Sis has got her head down; she's staring into her coleslaw. She's smart enough not to want to watch me squirm.

"Well, there's . . . Alex."

"Alex?" my mom brightly asks, as if somewhere in her mind she's writing it down. "Tell me about him."

"He's a nice guy. Lives just a few blocks over."

"Where'd you meet him?"

"Downtown, at the comic book store. I was flipping through some old issues of *X-Men* and he just came up and started talking to me, about the X-Men, I mean. We walked back to his place and played Sega for the rest of the day. Cool guy, really."

I've got no idea where all of this is coming from; I've never met a kid named Alex in my life. I've always liked the name, though, because it has an X in it – Xs and Zs (like in Zack) I always thought were cool to have in a first name, but not in a last name because then it looks and sounds so ethnic. No one wants to be ethnic any more.

"So, his house? Tell me about his house. Was it nice?"

"What?" I mumble, still chewing on a buttermilk biscuit that's salty and too dry. I'm hoping Mom will soon tire of this subject and move on to another topic. At this point, I would kill to know how *her* day was.

"His house. Alex's house. Was it nice? Does his mom work? Are his parents still married?"

"Divorced," I say, though this probably wouldn't have been a lie if I really had met a kid named Alex at the comic book store. Most kids' parents seem to be divorced nowadays. "Well, just separated, really. They're, you know, giving it a chance."

"Go on, go on. You said you met someone else. Who else? What's his name? Or," my mom stops speaking and begins to grin, "is it a *her*? A cute little *fe*male, perhaps?"

Sis can get me out of this. Just one word will do it, saving me from these stories that anyone in their right mind would recognize as lies. But there's just silence, so I continue. With the look in my mother's face – all bright and expectant – I have to.

"No, no, it's a guy, Mom. I haven't met a girl . . . yet." I think of the girl at the diner, Donna, whom I suppose I could talk about since it's true that I met her. I mean, at least she really does exist. But instead of blabbing all about it, I keep my mouth shut. I don't want to jinx it. "This guy . . . his name is . . . Roger. He's pretty cool. Lives one town over. He just came into Walther the other day for the hell of it. In his car."

"A car? He has a car?" My mother leans back and nervously runs her fingernails across the gold polyester blazer which she has not yet taken off since coming home. "Oh, Perry, I don't know. I don't know if I want you going around with a boy with a *car*."

She says the word "car" as if it were a kind of weapon whose sole purpose was to kill and maim. She has a car, Sis does, the whole goddamn world has a car except me.

"How old is this Roger?"

"Sixteen, I guess. I didn't ask. You told me it was impolite to go around asking people their age."

"Just when you meet a woman, I mean. You're not supposed to ask adult women, like my friends, for example, how old *they* are . . . but some stranger with a *car*, for heaven's sake, most definitely, *yes*. . ."

After a few more chews of her extra-crispy wing, my mom puts the almost picked-clean bone down to the plate and says, "Perry, I don't think I approve of you going around with someone who owns a *car*. I think you're too young. I'm sorry, but that's just the way it is."

This almost kills me, that she doesn't approve of one of my make-believe friends. Sometimes I think, no matter what you do, you're always going to be disappointing someone.

"But . . . Mom," I try to protest, but protest about what? For some reason I repeat the name, "Roger. . ."

"Roger can find friends his own age. And so can *you*."

"Yeah, yeah," I say, even though this is totally untrue. I *can't* find friends my own age. I can't find friends, period.

In fact, on Tuesday, while I was inside watching TV, someone stole my skateboard. It was in the garage, leaning against the far wall next to the door that leads into the house, and someone must have walked right up Sis's driveway, right into the garage – all the way in – taken my almost brand-new Santa Cruz skateboard, and run off. This was in the middle of the day and in broad daylight. I was so stunned by it that I haven't yet said anything to anybody. If I told Mom she'd just tell Sis and Sis would tell Bob and Bob's such a great guy he'd probably want to set up a house-to-house search looking for it, but that wouldn't help, even if we found it, because then the whole neighbourhood would want to kill me. I hate having this story inside me with no one to tell it to, but there's nothing else I can do.

Before Mom or Sis came home I tried to call Josh, thinking that out of all the people in the world, he might understand. Even though it was only six o'clock, and every time I talk to him he tells me about the long hours he works in Manhattan, I still thought it was worth a shot to try and catch him at home. Predictably, no one picked up until, after four rings, the machine did. *"Hi, you've reached Josh and Kendra's. . ."* It was her voice on the machine. Hearing Kendra's voice, after staring at her picture for the past couple of months, made me feel weird. It was as if a silent movie suddenly had sound. Just as she started saying something about leaving a message at the beep, I quickly slammed down the phone, feeling hot and a little flushed. Sometimes I'm happy that my brother found someone to marry; other times I wish he were still just a bachelor.

"Well, I'm sorry, Perry, but you'll do what I say." My mother takes the last sip of Coke from her plastic cup, and then rises and begins clearing the table. As she runs hot water over each of the plates, she turns to me and says, "You may not like it, but that's the way it is. I guess you'll just have to spend most of your time with Alex."

"Who?"

"Alex . . . the boy from the comic book store."

"What? Oh, yeah, *him*."

During my second week in Walther, I had trouble sleeping. It wasn't the bed; the bed was OK. And it wasn't the room, either. Bob had done a really nice job. The place was great, almost better than what I had before. The problem was that whenever I closed my eyes, all I could see was the past: our old house, the town I used to live in, my previous room.

I could still see our street. I could see it so vividly in my head that it was like the memory was a scene in a movie. The images were still so fresh in my mind that it was all as real as if it were right outside.

Sometimes I took tours of our suburb in Tucson in my imagination, as if I were a bird or a low-flying plane. I pictured myself gliding through the streets and going to all the old stores and markets we used to go to, ordinary places like the drugstore where I had my asthma medication filled and the pizza place my mom always took me to when I got good grades. In my mind I cruised in and out of it all, through the toy store and around the arcade.

But what left me feeling so strange and kept me up at night, was the fact that all of it was still there: the town, my friends, those places. I used to think of it all as a movie set, and that I was the star, and that without the star the sets would be dark and empty, a ghost town. But in these visions which kept me awake no matter how hard I begged my brain for sleep, what always made me feel sad was how life in my old town had continued right on without me. This made me feel like I hadn't made a difference at all, not a dent in anyone's life. They had all just forgotten me and moved on. My friends had made new friends, arcades were never in need of kids with quarters, and pizza places never have to look for hungry mouths. I wondered what the point of all of it was, if no one cared enough to remember.

And now here I was in yet another town, banging my head against a new wall, knocking on a strange door and trying to get someone to notice me. And it just wasn't working. I wondered how long I'd have to knock before someone came to take me away for making so much noise.

Bob came over last night, and he alone out of the three of them could tell that something was wrong. Neither Mom nor Sis seemed to be able to tell that I was lonely and hurting inside, but Bob could tell right away. I would say that it was because of some sort of emotional bond between us, but I didn't think that men had those kinds of feelings. Or maybe we do, but we're just too ashamed to admit it. Anyway, Bob left after dinner and then came back. He said he wanted to check on something in my room, to make sure he hadn't left any nails poking out on which I could seriously hurt myself, but I knew that that was just bullshit, and that he wanted to get me alone for some reason.

When he came back, he gave me a sort of notebook. It wasn't a notebook like you'd use for school, even though it had blank pages inside of it, like for taking notes in class. But this book was much nicer than that. Actually, it looked like a book you'd buy in a bookstore, like a novel or something. It was bound really well and had a hardback cover sheathed in black denim. There was even a length of satin sewn into the binding that was to be used as a bookmark.

"What is it?" I asked when he handed it to me.

"It's a blank book. Use it to write stuff down in. Your thoughts, feelings."

"You mean like a . . . *diary*?" I said the word in a way which implied that a diary was something just for girls.

"Call it a *journal*. Or don't call it anything . . . it's just a place where you can say whatever you want to."

I turned it over and over again in my hands. It really was nice. After he'd called it a journal and not a diary, everything was suddenly different. Now I could see myself actually using the thing.

This morning I wake up after again not sleeping very well, and I waste a couple of hours watching TV and lingering over my bowl of Fruit Loops until the cereal is too soggy to eat and the milk has turned all sorts of colours and is too warm to drink. When I see that it's one o'clock, I stuff the blank book Bob gave me (which, so far, is still blank) into a backpack, and decide to head down to Gus's Diner, to see if Donna's working today.

I haven't told anyone about Donna yet, not Mom or Sis or Bob or Josh when he called last week. I haven't told anyone because there's really nothing to tell. I know her name but she doesn't know mine, and the only reason I know hers is because it was on her nametag. After all, it's not like she stopped me in the street and introduced herself. If every time a boy had a crush on a girl and he got on the phone to tell the world about it, there would be nothing but ringing phones for the rest of eternity.

"Hiya, kid."

As I walk into Gus's, not only don't I find Donna, but I don't find anybody: the place is empty except for the cook who's leaning against the counter and a bus boy in the very back booth marrying the contents of various ketchup bottles with others so that they're all topped off.

"Oh, hi," I say, sort of taken aback at the intimacy of the situation. I mean, where is everybody? Not having enough sense to keep my thoughts to myself, I ask, "Where is everybody?"

"It's a little slow right now, what with people at work and most of the kids at camp or away vacationing or something."

The cook eyes me strangely, as if trying to figure out why I'm not on a vacation or at camp. I try to think of an excuse for about half a second, but then stop. After all, it's none of this guy's business why I'm stuck in Walther for the summer. I mean, I could ask him the same thing. Why isn't *he* on vacation?

"Will, uh, Donna be in later?"

He sort of keeps looking at me strangely, as if he can't quite place the name, so I add, "You know, Donna, the waitress?"

"What? Oh, sure. Yeah, kid, sorry. I guess I was day-dreaming. Yeah, she'll be here at four. I'm watching the counter until the next shift comes on. In the meantime, what can I getcha?"

I'm not really hungry because of the cereal I ate just a few hours ago, but I order a grilled cheese sandwich anyway, just so I'll have something to do, something to pick at. With a plate in front of me, I figure I'll look more natural when Donna finally arrives. After all, this is a diner and I'd look pretty stupid just standing around whistling.

I take the blank book Bob gave me out of my backpack. I look through the window between the grill and the counter space, and I can see that the cook's not smoking a cigarette this time, so I feel a little better and actually begin to get hungry. The smell of the buttered bread toasting on the griddle wafts through the air and into my nostrils, and then I hear the splatter of a fresh bag of frozen French fries being tossed into boiling oil. All of a sudden, I'm starving.

While I'm waiting one of the other waitresses, an older woman, comes in even though it's only three-thirty. She puts on an apron and handles the few tables which have become occupied since I entered the deserted diner just a few minutes ago. Maybe that's why the place was empty. No one likes to go into a restaurant if no one else is in there.

I sip on a Sprite and stare down at the bare, white pages of the journal, trying to think of something to write. None of the things Bob suggested I write about, like my thoughts or feelings, seem to be organizing themselves into words or paragraphs, so I can't really write about them. Then I think that instead of writing to myself, maybe I can write something to someone else, like a letter. I figure that I can write it in the book and then just rip out the page and pop it in the mail.

I think about writing a few letters to some of my

friends back in Tucson, or maybe even one or two to a couple of guys I used to hang around with in Portland and who I still think about from time to time.

It's funny but, every time I've moved, me and my friends have vowed to stay in touch, to write letters and keep each other posted on what we're doing, how school is, etc. But every time I've moved, that's never happened. I haven't received a single letter from one of those guys, and I've never written one to them myself. Maybe they've been waiting for me to write, and meanwhile I've been waiting for them, and all of us are waiting for the other person to make a move. But that's crazy. Someone's got to be first, and you'd think that out of all those friends there'd be just one who was willing to try. Friends say they'll write, that they'll keep in touch, but I've found that most often they don't; they just slowly drift away. Pretty soon weeks become months and months become years and then you can't remember why you liked them in the first place.

"Hey, old sport, you waiting for that pen to jump up and write all by itself?"

"What?"

"The page, that blank page. You're not going to get anywhere by just staring at it."

I hadn't even noticed, but while I was getting out my blank book and trying to decide who I should write a letter to, a guy and a girl had sat right next to me at the counter, which is odd since the rest of the counter, all twelve seats except mine, are unoccupied.

"Oh, I'm just sort of . . . you know . . . figuring out what to write."

"Sure, old sport, sure," he says, and moves from resting on the counter with his elbows to leaning back and letting out a huge sigh, as if he's bored by the whole world.

"Why do you keep calling me 'old sport', anyway?"

"What? Oh, I just read a novel where this one guy calls another guy 'old sport' for the entire book. Pretty cool, eh?"

It doesn't sound cool to me, it sounds annoying. After all, this guy's only called me "old sport" twice but already it's getting on my nerves. I can't imagine some-body calling me that for an entire book. Once again, not having enough sense to keep my mouth shut, I let my thoughts escape out of my mouth.

"No, that's not cool at all. Why did the guy call him 'old sport', anyway? Was he athletic or an old man or something?"

The kid sitting next to me suddenly turns silent. He has red hair and a face full of freckles, and his pale skin slowly becomes red with embarrassment as a suit-able smart alecky answer to my question eludes him. Since he's down, I figure I might as well kick him, because mercy's not something that kids care too much about – that's why we're always making fun of or bully-ing each other.

"I mean, how can you go around calling people 'old sport' if you don't know why this guy called this other guy 'old sport' in the first place? That just seems stupid to me."

For the first time since he got my attention, it seems like he doesn't know what to say. I bet this doesn't happen to him often. The girl sitting next to him, who also has red hair but not as many freckles, pokes him in the ribs with her elbow. I think she's his sister; his older sister. The look on her face seems to say, *I've been waiting for this moment for a long time.*

After a few more seconds roll by, he shakes off his embarrassment and offers his hand.

"Carter Hannon, my good man. It's not often I allow a stranger to get me tongue-tied like that, so I consider you a worthy adversary. And it's the smart soldier who turns any real foe into a friend. Don't you agree?"

His hand has been hanging out the whole time he's been saying this, but I was listening too closely to reach out and grab it, so when his little speech is over I finally drop my pen and shake his hand. Afterwards, he quickly drops his arm to the counter, as if it had greatly tired his arm to hold it outstretched for such a long time.

"Uh, yeah, I agree. My name's Perry. Perry Mathews. One T. Some people have two Ts but I've, uh, only got one."

"Well, I won't hold it against you."

After Carter says this the girl sitting next to him laughs, but not in a way that signifies she thinks anything was funny; it just seems like she wants attention.

"And this fetching beauty is my sister, Marina."

I reach across Carter's chest to shake her hand, even though the formality's not necessary. Carter's right, she is a beauty. She has short red hair and pale green eyes, and is wearing a tight black shirt with a wide neck, the fabric stretching over two broad shoulders. I'd say she's a few years older than me, but Carter looks like he's just about my age, if not younger.

"You're new around here, aren't you?"

"What? Oh, yeah." I sit back as the cook comes out from behind the grill to deliver my sandwich, which he gives me with a wink. "I just moved here."

"Really, old sport? Where from?"

"Tucson," I say.

"Arizona?" Carter asks, making the question sound as if I had said I'd just moved to Walther from Saturn or Mars. "So, what brings you out East, to the land of civilized folk?"

I'm thankful he keeps coming up with questions, because I'm not much of a conversationalist with people I don't know, which is another reason that meeting people for me is so hard. I never know what to ask that doesn't sound like job interview questions.

"Well, my mom just got divorced so we. . ." and with that I begin to tell him my story, except that I leave out the more depressing aspects of it and try to concentrate on the exciting adventure of moving to a new city where I don't know a soul, which is how my mom sold me on the idea last month.

As Carter and Marina listen to me talk, I watch their nodding heads and begin to think that maybe they believe what I'm saying. That's the great thing about meeting someone for the first time: you're allowed to create yourself as anything you want to be. Maybe they really can't tell that I'm scared shitless by all of this, or that this little monologue is the most I've spoken in over a month. Maybe I can fool them into thinking I'm OK.

A couple of times I pause in my story and push my plate of French fries towards Carter and his sister, motioning for them to help themselves. Every time I do this Carter's eyes sort of light up in an odd, interested way, as if he's never been shown such hospitality before. I can tell by the way they're dressed (in very expensive clothes that look brand new) that money is not a problem for either one of them. They can obviously buy as many French fries as they want, so the fact that I'm sharing my food with them seems to throw Carter for a loop. I think he's used to hanging around people who want something from him, not people who want to give him something.

"Hell of a story, old sport. Hell of a story."

The cook comes out from behind the grill again and drops off two white plastic bags. In one there are two drinks with straws already poking out of their lids, while the other smells like fresh hamburgers. The cook seems to regard Carter and Marina with a touch of suspicion, as if there's been bad blood between them before.

"Here you go, Hannons," the cook says, addressing

both of them at once, which I think is a neat trick. "Your usual."

Without even looking up, Carter pulls out an expensive-looking wallet and drops a twenty on the counter. What amazes me is the fact that his wallet is made of leather. What fourteen-year-old needs a leather wallet? Until you go to college, Velcro is just fine. Peering into Carter's wallet as he pulls out the bill, I can see that the twenty is just one of many.

"So, where do you live, old sport?"

"Over on Taylor."

"Hmmm," Carter says, looking at the ceiling as if considering something. "That's not too terribly far from us, is it, Marina?"

She slaps her brother on the shoulder.

"Oh, Carter, you *know* it's not."

"Well then, why don't you give me a call some time? Hannon. I'm in the book."

As soon as Carter finishes trying to be suave, Marina quickly picks up the bags of food and exits the diner, her brother following closely behind. They both get into a black BMW, with Marina behind the wheel, and in a matter of seconds they're gone.

Before I have a chance to think about whether or not I've just made a friend, Donna rushes into the diner, out of breath and looking haggard. Her hair is messy, clumsily drawn into a ponytail with strands popping out all over her head. Her uniform is wrinkled and hanging on her body all wrong, the collar lined with lace sticks up against her neck. It looks like it took her about four seconds to get dressed.

"You're late," the cook calls out from behind the grill, where he's started smoking a cigarette. As he begins to reprimand Donna for her tardiness, I begin to think that maybe this man is more than just the cook. Maybe he's also the manager, or even the owner. Maybe *he*'s Gus.

I can half hear Donna pledge numerous apologies as she stands in a little hallway in between two bathrooms and a door that leads into the back of the diner. The cook just sort of shrugs her off with numerous "*yeah, yeahs*", and when she reappears on the floor of the restaurant, she's smiling and tying an apron around her waist. I guess her excuse worked.

"That was a close one," she says in my ear as she takes two glasses of water to a couple that just sat down at a table near the entrance.

It takes a second for me to react to what she said – it's not the words that astound me, it's the fact that she remembered me. I have about a minute to think of a response since she's now started to take the couple's order, and then is stopped by one of the other waitress's tables on her way back towards the counter. By the time Donna returns, all I've managed to come up with is, "So, you were late, huh?"

"Yeah," she says, brushing aside the obvious idiocy of my question. "I was just right over there, in the square, reading, and time just got away from me. You know how it is when you're reading a *really* good book and days could've gone by and you'd still be there in that chair, reading that book?"

I don't quite know what she's talking about since I've never had a book affect me like that, but Donna's too beautiful to disagree with, so I just nod my head vehemently back and forth.

She fills up a couple more glasses, two with tea and one with Coke, and drops off the teas at the table near the entrance and the Coke at the other waitress's table. The other waitress — her name tag says HI I'M SHERRY — mouths Donna a "Thank you" when she comes out from behind the counter with her arm full of plates of food, and Donna responds with a similarly silent "You're welcome". Then she comes back around the counter and attaches her table's order to the silver wheel over the food window, and she gives the wheel just enough of a push so that her order spins right around and then stops in front of the cook's face. *This girl*, the thought pops into my head, *is perfect*.

As she pauses at the counter to make a new pot of coffee, I figure that this is my big chance. I've got to introduce myself right now and try and talk to her, invite her away from the diner where we can talk without her having to worry about delivering western omelettes and burger after burger.

"Look, Donna. . ." I say, but then chicken out.

My absence of courage gives her the time to ask, "How did you know my name?"

I motion to her name tag with a trembling finger.

"Oh, yeah. Duh. So, what's *your* name?"

"Perry. Mathews." Having wasted enough time as it is, I leave out the business about there only being one T in my last name and not two. Soon the diner will be filled with people and then the whole world will have her attention, but right now it's mine. "Look, this may sound crazy but I'd like to see you sometime. You know, when you're not working. Away from here, I mean. So we could just . . . talk."

I've never in my life asked a girl out before, but what I just said sounds about right. If I ever get up the courage to do it again, maybe those same words will come in handy. Meanwhile, I can see that Donna's weighing the decision in her head. Now, asking her out doesn't seem so difficult; it's the waiting for the answer that's going to kill me.

Finally she saves my life and says, "Sure."

She's waved over to one of her tables, but when she gets back she says, "My next day off is Wednesday. We can go out then. How does that sound?"

"Sounds great," I say, even though today is only Thursday. Wednesday feels like a million miles away. "Wednesday, yes."

"Great. Call me Tuesday night and we'll figure out where and when. OK? Here's my number."

She leans over me and takes the pen from where it's sitting in the crease of the book Bob gave me. In the three seconds it takes to write down seven numbers, I think I may die from inhaling her rosy sweet perfume which rises off the back of her neck, and if I do the coroner won't know what happened except that something inside of me burst. She drops the pen, smiles, and then goes back to work. Enveloped in equal parts happiness and shock I look down; the blank book is no longer blank. My God, even her handwriting is beautiful.

My walk home turns into a run because I'm so excited by the fact that not only do I have a date with Donna, but I also met Carter and his sister. Here I'd been knocking my brains out all week trying to make some friends, sneaking up on basketball games and generally wandering the streets like an idiot, and yet in one of the brief moments when I forgot all about meeting someone, I met someone.

When I told Mom and Sis about Carter and Marina, and then about Donna – about how I had made two friends and also got a date for next week – neither of them could believe it. Hell, I sort of didn't believe it myself.

At the dinner table they were both hysterical, asking all sorts of questions, especially about Donna. You would have thought I told them we were getting married instead of just going out on a date. Every time Mom spoke to ask me yet another question about any of my new acquaintances, her eyes lit up. And every time she listened to one of my answers, she just sat back in her chair and pleasantly sighed. I could tell that my mom had been aching for me to have a little good news.

I've known for a long time that if I'm not happy my mom can't be completely happy, and for years this has angered me, made me feel like I've got a huge burden on my back, like there's an added dose of responsibility always stalking me. I mean, when am I allowed to be down and depressed? Why does it have to depress her, too? But I guess that'll never change, because I'll always be her child. A parent's concern is a shadow you can never get out from under.

The funniest part of the evening was when Mom, Sis and I were done with all the celebrating, we turned off all the lights in the kitchen and the television set in the living-room which no one was even watching, and as my mom marched me to my room, she said, "But what about Alex and Roger?" I didn't say anything for a second, unable to place the names. Finally it hit me: Alex and Roger were the fake friends I had made up last week. My mother was so great to have remembered. I swear that somewhere she's got a list with everything about me written on it: when I first walked, when I first talked, what are my favourite foods, who all my friends are. I told her to forget about Alex and Roger. "I'm sure they'll get over it," I said.

I called Carter over the weekend, mainly just so I would have something to do to pass the time while waiting for my date with Donna on Wednesday. On Saturday morning I looked up his number, and his voice when he finally answered the phone was smug and assured, as if he'd been waiting for my call.

"Old sport," he began, "glad to hear from you. An honour, truly. Indeed."

The tone in Carter's voice was that I was a fish he had caught using the clever bait of his own charm, and that there was no question that I'd seek him out. I got the feeling that he wasn't used to people resisting him, but this couldn't be true because he wasn't necessarily a good-looking guy. Of course, he does have his sister, who has that car, and they both seem to have a lot of money and money, as even children know, talks.

Saturday afternoon we met downtown at Walther's one movie theatre, caught the film, and then walked around for a little while afterwards until he had to meet his sister and parents for dinner at a restaurant a few blocks away. He turned out to be pretty decent company, and was OK to talk to when he wasn't trying to impress me with all the places he'd been (too many countries in Europe to remember) or with all the things his dad had bought him (as soon as he turned sixteen he was going to get a BMW of his own). In fact, underneath all of his bragging and big talk, I began to detect a kid who was as scared of life and himself as I was, maybe even more.

On Sunday, Carter called and invited me out for a drive with him and Marina. I jumped at the chance, immediately accepting his invitation, but while waiting for him to arrive I regretted saying yes.

I knew that Sis's house wasn't much to look at – it wasn't even as nice as the one I used to live in back in Tucson – and I could only imagine what sort of mansion the Hannons lived in. I considered calling Carter back and having him and Marina pick me up on the corner instead of coming to Sis's door. But I didn't, and eventually Carter came in and even met my mother, who seemed to like him. Actually, I was a little sad to see Mom fall so quickly under the spell of his charm. I thought she was a keener judge of character than that. Or maybe she was going easy on him because she wanted me so badly to have a friend. At any rate, she was extra-polite to Carter and even offered him something to drink, which he – also being polite – declined.

Standing in the living-room, Carter issued the standard compliments, saying what a lovely house it was and how nicely it was decorated. I watched him, impressed by his overall smoothness. I wouldn't say I admired him, but he certainly did amaze me in a certain way.

Marina waited in the car the whole time, and when we finally came out her face was plastered with a look of complete boredom which didn't leave for most of the day.

I sort of got the feeling that her parents had forced her take Carter and I for the sightseeing trip through Walther's backroads, eventually travelling all the way out to the county line. Why she had even agreed to take us I couldn't be sure, except that maybe she knew she'd be bored anyway. A town like Walther was probably too small for a girl like Marina. I began to get the feeling that when she was just a girl she became a woman of the world.

At a little general store way out in the country we all stopped for ice-cream, and on the way back into town we played the radio loud and sang along to songs we knew. Every few minutes we'd lose the signal of one small radio station, so we'd tune in to another.

From the backseat, I watched her. Marina really was beautiful, and I liked her better than Carter. She seemed less affected by their family's wealth than he did, or maybe he just needed it more – not being as good looking as she was – but whatever the reason, she never tried as hard as Carter did to always be clever. Marina seemed more comfortable just being herself.

When Carter had to make a pit-stop halfway back to Walther, she and I were left alone in the car.

"So, *old sport*," Marina said, but I could tell by the way she pronounced the words that she was just using them to make fun of her brother. "How do you like Walther?"

When she said this I was looking through the BMW's sunroof, to the clear blue sky which stretched overhead. I hadn't expected her to say anything; I just assumed we'd sit in silence while Carter took his piss.

"Oh, uh, I guess it's . . . OK."

"Well, it's not paradise, that's for sure."

"How do *you* like it here, Marina?"

"It's all I know, really. What can I compare it to? I've lived here all my life. Same town, same friends, even the same room. But you, it sounds like *you*'ve been everywhere."

This made me laugh; it sounded like such a positive thing coming out of her lips.

"Yeah, but what about you? Yesterday Carter told me about how your family travels all the time. Different cities, all those countries."

"Big deal," she sighed. "We always come back *here*. Who cares where you go if this is what you come back to? Me, I'd like to leave and never come back. Now *that*'s the trick."

From behind the gas station Carter came hobbling out of the rest room, a few wet spots on the front of his beige shorts.

"I've done that before, Marina. The leaving and never coming back."

"Yeah? Is it fun?"

"Not as much as you think."

When he got in the car, Carter asked, "What'd I miss?" but Marina and I just grinned and ignored him.

As we drove back into town, I couldn't believe that the conversation between Marina and I had flowed as smoothly as it did. Normally I'm shy around strangers, or else intimidated by beautiful girls, especially older ones. But with Marina that all melted away, which is crazy because I know that if I were to have seen her in a crowd a week ago I never would have had the courage to say a damn thing.

By the time they dropped me off it was dark and I'd missed dinner, but I didn't care because I was full from the ice-cream and the thrill of spending most of the day with Carter and Marina. My mom didn't mind that I was late, either; she was just glad that I had finally made some friends. She knew it had been a while since I was that happy.

On Monday night I told her that for my date with Donna I wanted to wear this light blue linen shirt which I got as a Christmas present two years ago but which still fits. The only problem is, it's missing two buttons, which came off in the wash. I tried wearing it once anyway, hoping no one would notice, but for the entire day my white belly kept sticking out of the front of my shirt, which waved back and forth like a tent-flap.

Last night Mom told me she'd sew the buttons back on, and leave the shirt in Sis's sewing-room upstairs. She said she was tired, that it'd been a hard day, but that she'd get to it before going to sleep. She promised me all this with a very heavy sigh, as if she really didn't have time to do it but would do it anyway. It was another one of those nights where it was nine o'clock at night and she was still wearing that awful gold blazer. I swear, she's worked there just a couple of weeks and half her nights have been like that.

Tuesday morning, after I've slept late yet again and helped myself to a lingering bowl of Fruit Loops in front of the TV, I slowly climb the stairs towards the first story of the house, which I still have never been to even though I've lived here for almost a month now. In fact, I was shocked when Mom mentioned Sis's sewing-room, because I thought there were only two rooms up there, my mother's bedroom and Sis's, with a bathroom in between.

At the end of a short hallway the sewing-room is next to one of the bedrooms, I'm not sure whose. The bedroom door is closed and I don't want to open it to find out if it's Mom's or Sis's. I figure that's information I can do without.

The sewing-room is small, almost as small as my room, but not quite. Unlike most of the downstairs, which is carpeted, the sewing room's floor is made of wood, a dark brown stained wood which shows just how old the house is. The corner windows overlook the driveway and back yard, giving a clear view over a group of elm trees in Sis's back yard of half a dozen back yards belonging to the homes one street over. In the middle of the room is a rocking chair, and next to this is an antique sewing machine which is black with the word "Singer" in fancy script lettering on the side in gold paint. Under the window there's a table filled with spools of thread, spools of yellow measuring tape, and a pin-cushion with an elastic strap which, I guess, goes around Sis's wrist.

Draped over one of the arms of the rocking chair is my blue shirt. I grab the shirt and turn to leave, except something catches my eye. What stops me is a full-length mirror which sits on the floor, leaning against the wall. The gigantic thing is housed in an ornate wooden frame painted silver. This must be an antique, and it reminds me of just how old some of the stuff in this house is, in this whole town, for that matter. Walther is ancient compared to the places I lived before, like Tucson or Portland. Nothing in America is as old as the East Coast, except the Indian stuff that was here before, but nobody really cares about that.

I stand in front of the mirror, turning around to see myself from various angles, the way Sis probably does before every date with Bob. It's funny though because I don't know if it's the way this mirror is tilted or something else, but it makes me look like a spider: all legs. Even though I'm wearing a pair of jeans and a T-shirt, most of my body looks like it's covered in blue denim, but that can't be right. Can I really be *this* tall?

I tuck my shirt in and then stand at a right angle towards the mirror, then the left. For once in my life I don't hate what I see. I actually don't look that bad. In fact, if I saw myself walking down the street, I'd think I was a pretty cool guy. This is a shock to me because I've never much liked mirrors. Mirrors for me have always been like that loud-mouthed friend that insists on telling the truth when you wish they'd just shut up. Some truths don't need to be spoken, like how bad I am at math or that I can't catch or throw a baseball. I know all of those things and I don't need someone around to tell me. That's how I've always felt about mirrors, that they were just big mouths telling me how ugly I am. But today, right now, looking into this one, I feel OK.

Maybe it's just the angle, or even this mirror (like the way the ones at the carnival make you look fat, Sis's mirror makes me somehow look good), or maybe it's that

I'm looking forward to seeing Donna tomorrow. Maybe it's just hope that has somehow made me handsome. I hope not, because that means that if things don't go well with Donna, I go back to being ugly again.

For our date, Donna asked me to meet her on the steps in front of the library, which I thought was strange since we both live so close to each other and were probably going to have to take the same bus into town. I guess she just didn't want any awkwardness to come so soon in the evening, sitting side by side on a creaking bus with all those old people staring at us and listening to our conversation. When other people are around, it's always hard to talk to someone you don't know very well.

Still, her decision disappointed me because I was looking forward to going to her house to pick her up, to ringing her doorbell and getting that first look at her when the door was swung wide open, like the way the curtains go up at a Broadway show. Or maybe her dad would have opened the door, and he and I would have chatted for a few minutes while Donna was upstairs getting ready. Her father and I could have just rolled our eyes and said under our collective breath, "Women."

Of course I get to the library early, way early; almost a half-hour before we're supposed to meet. When I spoke to Donna last night she was so casual about the whole thing she said we should meet on the steps "around seven", which I'm now thinking could be from anywhere between seven o'clock and eight. I could be out here half the night by myself.

Despite the hot day, the temperature has cooled off nicely, and there are clear skies and an icy breeze whistling through Walther. It's still pretty light out, since it's late June and summer only officially began last week. The sunset won't happen for another hour and a half. The days are so long lately that they drive me crazy; there's nothing worse than a long day when you're lonely, because you just want that day to end.

From where I'm perched on the library steps, I watch the cars slowly circle the town square, pulling in and out of the parking spaces in front of the various shops. Then I turn my attention to the pedestrians wandering around the neatly manicured square, some stopping to sit at a bench or else stooping over for a mouthful of warm water from one of the four drinking fountains.

On the far left corner I can see a white glow coming from the window of Gus's Diner, customers going in and coming out. One of the customers leaving seems a little familiar, and as I watch the figure get larger and larger as they cross the street and begin walking through the square towards me, I realize that it's Donna.

"Hey," she says, her voice carrying easily in the clear, empty air.

"Hey," I call back, but in a normal voice since now she's standing right beside me.

"Sorry I'm late."

"Oh, are you? I hadn't noticed. I just got here myself."

She grins, knowing that this is a lie. She probably thinks I slept here.

"Did you just come from the diner?"

"Yeah, sorry. The manager called and needed me to take a lunch shift since Sherry, who was supposed to come in, had to be at home with her son who got sick last night."

Donna sits down on the steps so I sit down, too.

"Really? Is Sherry's kid OK?" The only reason I ask is because I think this'll make me look like a nice guy in Donna's eyes.

"Yeah, I guess. Turned out just to be a virus. But he was up all night, and his throat was so swelled he couldn't even swallow. Sherry thought he'd been bit by a spider or something."

"What did his dad think had happened?"

"Who knows? His dad's in Maryland. They were divorced a year after he was born."

"Yeah," I say, kicking at the limestone steps, "there's a lot of that going around."

Donna takes a large canvas bag from her shoulder and sets it on the ground. Peeking out of the almost-closed zipper I see a tuft of her yellow uniform. Instead of that outfit she's wearing a beige v-neck T-shirt and a pale blue skirt that's short and matches my shirt. On her feet are tan leather sandals which expose her toes, the nails of which must have been painted red weeks ago but now are just splattered here and there with colour. She looks really nice, beautiful in fact, but I'm afraid to tell her because it'll just sound so standard, like it's what I'm supposed to say.

"Listen, I hope you're not too tired to do something tonight. I mean, after having to work today."

"No, no," she says, though the second she starts to speak her words are interrupted by a yawn, which seems to confirm my suspicion that she *is* too tired. "Really, I'm OK. I've got tomorrow off instead of today, so it's no big deal."

"You sure?"

"Jeez, Perry, *yes*. I'm sure."

I don't know why, but I almost wanted her to say that she *was* too tired, that she just wanted to go home and end the evening now. Maybe we would have rescheduled, maybe we wouldn't have. I'm too nervous to care. In fact, I'm so nervous that I'm going to mess this up I'd rather not even try because if it doesn't work out — if she doesn't like me how I like her — I'll be totally disappointed. But if I can get out of this situation right now, I'll never know and my heart will never be broken.

"So then, since you're not too tired, what do you want to do. Hungry?"

"After staring at food all day — not to mention the food at Gus's — eating's the last thing on my mind."

"Yeah, me neither. I mean, I'm not hungry either."

"Hey, a new movie opened last week at The Walther. I think the next show starts at eight. Want to check it out?"

"Sure," I say, even though what's playing is the same

film I saw with Carter on Saturday, and it wasn't such a good film then. But I don't say anything because it's what Donna wants to do, and I'm starting to get the feeling that I'll do anything she wants. I'll sit in a room and watch paint dry as long as she's sitting there beside me in a skirt like she's wearing right now.

During the movie I consider holding her hand, but both of hers are already clasped, sitting in her lap. In order to touch some part of her body, I elbow her arm during the film's funny parts, and grab on to her shoulder during the fiery climax, where the director felt the need to blow up not only three cars and two buses but also a whole bridge in Manhattan. Poor Manhattan: it's always getting destroyed in the movies. The whole world loves to see New York City get trashed – as if all those rich, artsy neurotics were finally getting what they'd deserved for years.

After the movie I try to hold her hand heading up the aisle, but just with the little heels on her sandals she's taller than I am, so her hand hangs slightly above mine and this makes me uneasy so I let it go. Donna doesn't notice any of this – she's still thinking about the film as we head outside into the cool night, where the sun has disappeared and light has been replaced by dark.

"Let's go through the square. It's beautiful out. Have you ever seen the way they light up Alec at night?"

As we run across the street and into the square, Donna grabs my hand.

"Alec?" I ask, wanting to pull my hand away, but I don't. "Who's that?"

"Alec *Walther*, you big dummy."

Donna expertly leads me through the many trails to the centre of the square, where that pale green statue I've now seen dozens of times stands on a podium, lit up from various lamps and two spotlights at the statue's base. Donna sits down on a bench directly in front of the statue, and for a few minutes doesn't say anything. She just sits, then looks up, staring.

I look up, too, staring at the figure with the long face, receding hairline and thin moustache. For the first time I notice that the statue is made up of various parts welded together: the arms, legs and head are all attached to the trunk of his body.

"So, uh, who's that?" I finally say, just to break her out of the trance I think she's falling into.

"Alec Walther."

"Walther? Like the town?"

She turns at looks at me dumbly.

"Yes, like the town."

"Oh, did he found the town? Settled it, like? Way back when?"

"Nah, it's nothing like that. The town's been here since the mid-seventeen hundreds. It used to be called New Rockland, I think. Most people can't even remember the old name, and I guess I'm one of them. It was changed around the turn of the century."

"So then, who was this Walther guy?"

"Alec Walther was a poet and essayist. He was also one of the first transcendentalists, along with Thoreau and Emerson. Then he moved to New Rockland and began to write sketches about the territory, the kinds of pieces that are usually called 'local colour'. You know, describing all the little ways people lived back then, all of the strange customs and rituals of the area. Folk tales, stuff like that."

"Oh, yeah, sure. Folk tales," I say. Inside, I'm kicking myself for not listening more in school. I figure that understanding a phrase like "transcendentalism" would go a long way towards making Donna like me, but I can't remember a single thing.

"I guess you could say that Alec Walther was New Rockland's version of Washington Irving – the guy who wrote about Sleepy Hollow – except Walther's work never really caught on outside his home town. I guess there's such a thing as being *too* specific a writer, you know? Like, if you write stuff that only a handful of people can understand, then you'll never have more than a handful of readers."

"That would suck," I say, just trying to stay in the conversation.

Not taking her eyes off Alec's pigeon-shit encrusted face, Donna says, "I hope that doesn't happen to me."

"What? Oh, you mean, you write?"

"*Try* to write. I try, but it's . . . hard. To stare at that blank computer screen. Day after day." Donna, trying to convey just how much the thought frightens her, shakes her body like she's got the chills.

I want to say that I understand, that I still haven't filled a page of that blank book Bob gave me weeks ago. I want to tell her that I can't imagine writing anything like a whole book; filling one page is hard enough. But I don't tell her any of this because I'm afraid she'll think I'm being condescending, as if trying to scribble letters to my old friends back in Portland or Tucson is the same thing as what she's doing.

"What kind of writer do you want to be?"

"A novelist. A *great* novelist. Like a female F. Scott Fitzgerald, or Thomas Wolfe. I mean, those guys had passion, and they weren't macho assholes like Hemingway and Mailer."

I'm thinking, *Hemingway and who?*

"I want to write books that really matter. Novels that make people know they're not alone. I mean, that's why *I* like to read, so I know *I'm* not alone. To know that there are other people out there who feel the same way I do. It's a hell of a thing to sit in bed at night and think you're the only person in the world who's feeling that scared at that very second. But wouldn't it be great to know that someone else had once felt that bad? And that things just might be OK?"

"I never really thought of it like that before, but yeah."

Even though what she's saying makes a lot of sense, I'm instantly sidetracked from my thoughts when she reaches up with both of her hands and sweeps her long strawberry-blonde hair off the back of her neck, placing it on top of her head.

I can't take my eyes off her exposed shoulders and white neck, both of which are delicately lit up from the glow of the tall black lamps situated around Alec, Donna and I. Of all the naked pictures I've seen of women in magazines – of all the parts of their bodies that I'm supposed to like – not one bit of their exposed anatomy has done to my insides what just staring at Donna's bare neck and soft shoulders are doing to me right now.

"Donna," I start to say, "I really like you, and—"

But she cuts me off by quickly placing an arm around my neck and pulling my face towards hers. It takes me a second to realize what's happening, but then it hits me: a kiss.

Her mouth clumsily meets mine, then Donna's lips – which I can tell are chapped – slowly separate and I feel the scratchy tip of her tongue which pries apart my own lips, looking, I guess, for my tongue. As our heads keep moving around, giving our kiss all kinds of angles, our noses constantly bump into each other in a fun sort of way.

Having responded to the shock of what's happening, I untangle my arms from my side and put them around her, pulling her into me and caressing that neck which was driving me crazy just a few minutes ago. I feel sort of funny doing this in public, writhing around on a park bench like this, but we're just kids – we live with our parents – so it's not like we've got anywhere else to go. We don't even have the back seat of a car, not yet at least.

Donna finally pulls away, so I remove my arms from where they've settled around her waist. She looks at me, smiles, and then looks up at the statue. It's a nice moment that I don't want to ruin with words so, for once, I don't. We just sit there in silence for a while, until she looks at a thin silver watch on her wrist.

"Jeez, Perry, I've got to go."

"What? Oh, yeah. OK. Uh, can I walk you home?"

"Sure, but can we stop by Gus's first? I want to see how Sherry's doing. Make sure everything's OK with her son. It should take just a few minutes."

"No problem," I say as we get up and begin to head south, moving in the direction of the diner and away from the library steps where we met a few hours ago.

It's late – almost eleven – so the diner's practically empty. There are just a few customers finishing up desserts and cups of coffee. Just as we're going inside, I see a black BMW that looks familiar pull into one of the angled parking spaces.

I stand off to the side as Donna begins to talk to Sherry, but both of them are interrupted when Carter walks in and stands between them, barking out an order to Sherry without saying "Excuse me" or waiting for a pause in their conversation. I watch as Sherry warily writes down the order, but I'm at the other end of the room so I can't hear exactly what it is. It's probably just the usual: a couple of cheeseburgers, fries and shakes. There are fast food places all over Walther where Carter could get this kind of stuff at a drive-thru without even having to get out of the car, but I guess he always likes to make a scene. Sherry posts the order on the wheel in the food window, then goes back to talking with Donna. Donna gives her a hug, and then Sherry grabs a tote bag from underneath the counter, puts on a red MetLife windbreaker, and then quickly leaves. When Donna comes over to where I'm standing, her entire face is white. After our kiss her skin was flushed, pink like a strawberry, but now she looks like a ghost.

"Turns out Robbie –"

"Robbie?"

"Sherry's kid. Turns out he responded badly to the antibiotics they gave him, so now they're trying to figure out what else to do. Sherry's on her way to the hospital right now."

"Hospital?"

"Yeah, that's where they had to take him. Sherry's mom was watching him and got all freaked out when his whole face started puffing up." Donna pauses, looking like she might cry.

I'm just about ready to comfort her, put my arm around her or something, when Carter walks up to the both of us. Once again, he doesn't wait for an opening in the conversation, he just barges right in.

"Good evening, old sport. How does this night find you?"

"Fine, Carter, fine. What's up?"

"Nothing much. Just getting a little midnight snack for Marina and myself."

As if on cue, outside the diner the BMW's lights flash on and then off and the horn is honked three times. Jesus, doesn't anybody in this family have some patience or manners?

"Hey, Hannon, here's your order."

The cook comes from behind the grill and places the usual duo of white plastic bags on the counter.

Carter nods and then heads towards the food, looking somewhat disappointed. I'm sure he wanted to say something to Donna, but I have absolutely no idea whether he would have tried to make me look either good or bad in her eyes. He picks up the bags and makes to leave, except the cook gruffly calls after him.

"Fourteen-fifty."

"Oh," he stops and says innocently, "I paid Sherry for all this when she took the order."

The cook just stands there, his balled-up fists on each hip.

"Come on, Hannon. Fourteen-fifty. Just pay me so we can close and I can go home."

"Sir," Carter says, though the formality is really a veiled insult. I know that Carter doesn't think the cook deserves to be called *sir*. "I told you, I paid the waitress already. Why, I have a witness."

He turns and looks at me. So does Donna, and then the cook. I just stand there, motionless. When I don't speak, Donna does.

"Come on, Hannon, you did *not* pay Sherry. I was standing right next to her since before you came in until after she left, and all you did was tell her what you wanted. You *didn't* pay her, and you know it."

Instead of answering Donna, or even looking at her, Carter's eyes are still trained on me. Now my chest is beating even faster than it had earlier this evening, when Donna kissed me, and I thought I was about to die then. I can tell that Carter's waiting for me to back him up, but at the same time Donna's waiting for me to tell the whole world just how full of shit he is. To me, none of this makes sense. What could Carter be thinking? There's no way his excuse can last. Sherry will be in tomorrow, or the next day, and then his whole story will fall apart and everyone will find out.

"Perry, old sport, will you tell them? Will you *hurry up* and tell them, before this wretched repast gets cold and it's not even worth eating much less digesting?"

"I-I-I don't know," I finally say; it's all I can say. I'm too terrified to utter anything else. Now we're the only people left in the diner and it's deathly quiet. "I really wasn't paying attention. I mean, I was just standing back here, so I didn't . . . I mean, I really *couldn't* . . . see anything."

"You see?" Carter quickly says, jumping on the end of my words. "No one knows what really happened . . . except, that is, *me*. And I told you already and I'm not going to say it again. So I'm taking this food and I'm leaving."

Carter picks up the bags from where he set them down during the confrontation, and then leaves the diner without a word from anybody else. The cook just shrugs his massive shoulders, grabs a toothpick from the dispenser near the cash register, and begins gnawing on it with a sullen resignation. Outside, the BMW's lights come on, then the engine roars to life, and with a screech of tyres meeting the pavement, disappears.

Donna turns slowly, and when her eyes finally reach mine, they're bloodshot with impending tears. But I know that she's not going to cry out of sympathy for Sherry and little Robbie with the ballooned-out face; instead, she's about to burst with the anger she feels towards Carter and the cowardice she just saw in me. Without a word she walks out of the diner, crosses the street, and in a matter of seconds I can't find her blue skirt in the black night. She's gone.

july

Even though the Fourth of July was yesterday, some kid down the block decides to wake up the whole neighbourhood with what sounds like half a dozen firecrackers tossed into a trash can. I can hear him and a few friends laughing as they all run from the scene, heading into one of their houses to hide, while the trash can rolls down the street with a metallic clank.

The pop of the very first firecracker yanked me instantly from sleep, and the whip-crack of the next five dragged me permanently from a great dream which I knew there'd be no way to get back to, even if I somehow managed to go back to sleep.

I look at the plastic clock next to my bed and, after figuring out the significance of the big hand and the short hand (digital clocks have ruined everyone), I can tell that it's past noon and not really morning any more. Still, that doesn't mean some kid has to go around lighting fireworks. That's what yesterday was for.

I go into the kitchen and discover that, except for the ringing in my ears, the house is completely silent. Because of the holiday – it had been a long weekend – I guess I got accustomed to having both Mom and Sis around the house, and I wasn't expecting the emptiness of this morning. I guess I was counting on both of them still being here today.

For the past three days Mom made Sis and I breakfast. The first day it was French toast, then she made omelettes, and then yesterday, to finish off the jumbo pack of eggs she'd bought, we had omelettes again. My mom also cooked dinner twice, which hasn't happened once since we moved here. Usually we just ate fast food burgers or fried chicken or had a pizza delivered, but on Friday night she made stuffed peppers and Sunday she made another one of my favourites: lasagna. I'd almost forgotten how much I loved my mother's lasagna.

For the Fourth, Bob came over and he and I lit fireworks on the lid of one of Sis's trash cans. Throughout the afternoon and night we sent maybe a dozen missiles screaming and sparkling almost fifty metres into the air. Mom wasn't too crazy about the fireworks, but Bob said they were left over from last year and he just wanted to get rid of them. I didn't buy that for a second. I knew it was a lie, that he'd bought them last week, but either my mother believed him or else she backed down because she could see how much fun I was having.

Either way, she tried to act like she didn't care when-ever Bob and I went into the street to aim another firework at the clear blue sky. (Though she did make sure I had all of my fingers every time I returned. This didn't work on Bob though because, being a woodshop teacher, he'd already lost the tip of a thumb to a jigsaw years ago.)

While we were outside on the sidewalk, trying to light the string-like wick of a brick of firecrackers, Bob asked me about the book.

"Have you written anything in it yet? The one I gave you?" The look on his face was slightly mischievous.

"Oh, you mean the . . . journal?"

"Yeah."

"No, not yet," I had to admit.

"Really? Why not?"

"I don't know, it's just . . . the feelings you talked about, the stuff I should be putting in there . . . I mean, it's all there, inside me. It's just, I can't make it come out."

Suddenly I thought of Donna, of the books she wanted to write and the emotions she was going to have to get in touch with in order to produce those books. I couldn't imagine opening up my heart or my head like that for the whole world to see.

"Don't worry about it, Perry," Bob laughed. "You shouldn't have to drag anything out of yourself. The point isn't just to put something down on the page, or to fill up the book. The point is to understand *what* you're putting down, because what you're going to end up understanding is your*self*."

After he said this Bob turned back to the task of lighting the firecrackers and, in the flickering glow produced each time he lit a match only to see it blown out by the warm wind, I got a good look at his face. His looks were I guess what you'd call *rugged*; he had coarse hair, steely blue eyes and sun-tanned skin which looked sort of leathery; if he lived out west he might have ended up a cowboy or worked on an oil rig, instead of spending every day in front of students standing in wood shavings. The more time I spent with him, the more I liked him, and I could easily see why Sis was with him. But he didn't have any kids (neither did Sis), and as in love as Sis and Bob seemed, they never talked of marriage and he was only at the house a couple of times a week. I couldn't understand it. There must be a problem in there somewhere, but you certainly couldn't tell just by looking at them. But I guess that's always the case: just because a couple looks happy doesn't necessarily mean they are.

For dinner that night we barbecued the usual things: hamburgers, hotdogs, and chicken for Sis since she's not too hot on red meat. After dinner we played board games, and Bob snuck me half of his beer. It really was one of the best Fourth of Julys I can remember having, and it was certainly the best day I'd had in a long time. Together, the four of us felt like a family, and I didn't want any of it to end – the feeling, the day – even though

I knew it would. It was fun while it lasted, but for me it just didn't last long enough.

I haven't spoken to Donna since that night in the diner. Believe me, it's not because I haven't tried, because I have. I called her seven times the next day, but didn't speak to her once. Three times I got the family answering machine, and twice each parent told me she wasn't home. I did the same thing the next day, except then the phone just rang and rang. Finally, on Monday, the machine was hooked back up, so I left several messages but she never returned my calls.

I was surprised her parents didn't make her call me back out of basic politeness, but then I imagined all of the rotten things she'd probably told them about me. All of a sudden the house's silence made sense. In fact, I was calling so much that her parents were probably becoming afraid of me, starting to think I was some kind of stalker or psycho. After leaving a message on Tuesday, I haven't called her since.

I did, however, go down to Gus's to talk to her in person. While I didn't like the idea of ambushing her in public like that, I couldn't see any other way to get her to speak to me.

She wasn't working the day I went, there was just that older waitress that I remember had the sick kid, the one Donna had been so concerned about. Somehow her child's name floated to the surface of my overheated brain: *Robbie*.

Sherry told me that Donna had quit the previous

weekend. She hadn't given any sort of explanation, she just quit. While Sherry was telling me this, I could see that the cook was eavesdropping on our conversation and, through the window between the counter and grill, he shot me dozens of dirty looks. Because of Carter, I was losing friends all over Walther. But at least Sherry was nice to me, which made me think she hadn't heard the story of what happened that night in the diner, although I knew she must have.

Before I left, but after I thanked her, I asked her how Robbie was, and she seemed honestly touched by the question. She got a little teary and told me that her son's swelling had finally gone down, and that he was now feeling much better. I knew that my concern would make me look like a good kid in her eyes and that if she ever spoke to Donna again, she'd put in a good word for me.

As I was leaving Gus's, I remembered that when I talked to Donna on the phone the night before our date, she told me what street she lived on. The only reason she told me was because I'd asked. I was planning on picking her up, but then she began with all that business about insisting we meet on the steps of the library.

Leaving Gus's after talking to Sherry, I decided to head over to Donna's house. I knew that it was probably a stupid idea, and that she just might slap me when she found me standing on her doorstep, but if it was a crazy thing to do, then it matched how I was feeling inside. I really was desperate to talk to her. I wanted to try and explain how I had let things go wrong and to promise that if she gave me another chance, none of it would happen again. But most of all, I wanted to get over the hurdle of the countless apologies I'd have (and was willing) to make, because I craved having her back as a friend. I *needed* her. Selfishly, I just wanted to see her again; to *look* at her. If I had a million dollars I would have spent it just to see the back of her neck, or her smooth white knees below the hem of that blue skirt.

After finding her street, I roamed up and down the block, searching for the word *Early* on the mailboxes. Donna Hall Early, that's her full name. Finally, almost at the corner, the second house from the end had a plaque hanging above the front door that announced THE EARLYS.

I rushed up the steps and, without thinking of what I would say if someone answered, I knocked on the door several times. I stood there for five minutes, knocked again, and waited another five minutes. No one was home. At least, no one answered the door, though I sort of suspected someone was inside. I don't know why I thought this, it was just a suspicion. I figured that they all couldn't be gone all the time, every time I called and this moment when I decided to come over.

When I left the house, I was sure at least one pair of eyes, probably Donna's, was watching me sulkily walk away. I crept up the street, not knowing if I'd ever talk to her again.

I did, however, talk to Carter. He called the day after it all happened, early in the morning, and wouldn't you know but he acted as if nothing strange had occurred the night before.

"Want to see a movie?" he asked, his voice normal, sounding even a little bit bored.

I couldn't believe it. He was ready to just carry on as if nothing had happened. I'm sure I could have gone to the movie and he would have never mentioned the awful position he'd put me in. Instead, I had to bring it up. I didn't want to, but I knew that he never would.

"Why, Carter? Why'd you do it?"

"Do what, old sport?"

"Cut the crap, Carter, and just tell me."

He laughed, sounding sort of embarrassed, as if his hand had been caught in a cookie jar.

"Oh, relax. I was just trying to have a little fun. What are you getting so upset about? I go into Gus's all the time. Next time I'll pay the big ape double. It's no big deal, trust me."

"But what about Donna?"

"Who?"

"Donna," I repeated.

"Oh, *the girl*. What about her?"

"She won't call me back, thanks to you. She probably thinks we were in on it together. That it was something we planned."

"Yes, Mathews, it was the Great Burger Heist!" Carter started to laugh loudly. "Come one, come all, hear all about it! We'll be legends, I tell you. Why, we're a regular Bonnie and Clyde – I won't say who's who."

"Shut up, Carter, I mean it. I really liked her."

"What, and now you don't?"

"No, I still do, it's just . . . *she* doesn't like *me*. I can't get her to talk to me. She won't let me explain. The whole situation is really screwed and it's all because of. . ."

For some reason my voice trailed off and I was unable to complete the sentence. What I had intended to say was, *And it's all because of you.* But I stopped because I had the feeling that Carter didn't care about his role in my downfall or anybody else's. As long as he was happy – that's what was important. In fact, the more responsibility I gave him in driving a wedge between Donna and I, the more proud of himself he'd probably be. There's a little bit of the devil in all of us, but there was a lot of the devil in Carter.

"It's all because of *what*, old sport?"

"Nothing. Don't worry about it. So, why'd you call? What do you want?"

"The movie, remember?"

"Remember? I saw it again last night. I know it by heart – or should I say *stomach*. Forget it, I'm not seeing that movie for a third time. Besides, I don't feel like doing much today. I'll call you after the weekend, OK?"

"Suit yourself."

And with that, Carter hung up. He didn't offer an apology or even say "Goodbye". All he said was "Suit yourself".

By the time I called him back, it was July. Somehow, I'd managed to get through June. Now there was just

July to get through, and then August, and then high school would finally start, and if what everyone was telling me was true, then the next four years would be just a blur.

I could tell that Carter was glad to hear from me again. He tried to hide his enthusiasm, as if he never needed anybody else to have a good time, but I could hear in his voice how happy he was that I'd called. In fact, he invited me to his house for the Fourth, but I told him I had plans and that maybe we could do something the day after. I knew he wasn't happy about this – him always hating to be disagreed with – but he agreed anyway. Despite all of his confidence, I was beginning to think that he needed me just as much as I needed him. We were both outcasts.

At first I was embarrassed with the idea of inviting him over, of having Carter inside Sis's meagre little house again, but it was just too hot out to even consider the idea of going all the way across town to where he lived. So when he volunteered to ride his bike over and spend the afternoon just hanging out, there was no way I was going to say no.

By the time he shows at Sis's house, it's almost two and over a hundred degrees outside. Yesterday it was only about eighty, but today the weatherman's saying it'll be the hottest day of the summer. Because of this, Carter and I are just sitting in the den, watching TV, flipping channels and making fun of whatever show or commercial or video we land on.

"Say, next week's the big week, huh, old sport?"

It takes me a second to react to what Carter says, but then I figure out he's talking about my trip. Mom finally convinced Josh to let me come down and spend a week with him and Kendra. I overheard my mom's side of the conversation last week, and she kept saying, "Josh, don't be selfish. He *needs* this. Josh, don't be selfish. *Please. . .*" To hear her talk, I was waiting for someone to donate a kidney. But it worked. Josh gave in to his mother, like most boys eventually do, and the next day she bought my MetroNorth ticket for New York City. I leave this Saturday at three in the afternoon, getting into Manhattan at a little after six.

"Yeah, big week. Trip and all."

"You ever been?"

"What, to *New York*?" I say this as if I've been to New York as many times as I've been to the bathroom. "Sure. Of course."

"Hell of a city, isn't it?"

I eagerly nod my head, as if it would hurt me to agree more.

"We have an apartment there, you know. Well, my father and someone else from his firm. We all share it, his family and ours. It's sort of like a time-share."

"Time-share, yeah," I say, even though I have no idea what a *time-share* is.

"We go into the city every once in a while for the weekend, or to see the Christmas show at Rockefeller Center. You know, all of those fat Rockettes throwing their legs around. And we always spend New Year's Eve at The Plaza. It's sort of a tradition."

Listening to Carter talk about his family's wealth while he picks at a bare patch on the arm of Sis's faded Laz-E-Boy recliner, I begin to feel uneasy. To mask my shame, I just sort of laugh, as if I've done twice everything he's ever done. But I can tell that he doesn't believe me, that he's aware that I've never been anywhere except all of the sorry cities and states my mom has dragged me to over the years in between the various divorces and stepdads.

"Maybe you'll meet a nice female while you're down there, yes? And she'll take your mind off the fair Donna."

"Yeah, well, we'll just see about that. I mean, I doubt it . . . that's not really why I'm going. I'm going to spend time with Josh – that's all."

"Sure, I hear you, old sport. Heaven for*bid* you meet some nice little cutie outside the Waldorf and you two crazy kids go up to her suite and she pops *your* cherry. No, it'll be much more fun to go to the Bronx Zoo with your Big Brudder."

Rather than even try to convince him that I'm not a virgin and that my cherry was popped years ago, I stay silent, nervously chewing on my bottom lip. Carter always knows what to say: the wrong thing. Now he's got me thinking of Donna, and thinking of her and how she won't speak to me or see me makes me think of Carter and his role in all of this.

When we spoke on the phone the day before the Fourth of July, we talked again about that night in the diner. Carter didn't want to, but I forced him. He really did think that he was innocent, and that the whole thing was just a big joke that, for some unknown reason, only he found funny. It was all just somebody else's problem.

I asked him how Donna even knew who he was, since he's too young to go to Walther High. When I said this, Carter laughed hard and then admitted that he'd never gone to a public school in his life, and that he'd never even seen Donna until the beginning of this summer — the day he first saw me. When his chuckling finally ended, Carter told me that he'd gotten kicked out of prep-school last semester, though he wouldn't tell me exactly why, and that his parents — running out of ideas — would be sending him soon to Walther High.

He told me that the school he got kicked out was named Pencey Prep, and the tone in his voice led me to believe that it was the latest in a long line of schools just like it that Carter had been unceremoniously thrown out of. His parents, of course, weren't happy about this, and decided to make him pay for his behaviour. For the first time in four years, he wouldn't be spending part of his summer in Europe. But his real punishment was to come in the fall, when Carter was made to attend, for the first time in his life, public school. It was either that or enrol in a military academy down south where the students were still hazed and one or two a year died under the harsh treatment. He told me that he still tossed and turned at night, wondering if he'd made the right decision. After all, public school might be just as dangerous.

"That still doesn't explain how she knew you," I asked over the phone.

"I'm a Hannon," he replied slowly, as if he were not only bored of our conversation but was bored with being a Hannon. "Everyone knows who we are. Can I help it? Anyway, just forget about her. There's plenty more where she came from, trust me."

But I didn't trust him, and I couldn't forget about her.

Now he's leaning forward in the recliner, a devilish look on his face.

"What's with you?" I ask. "Why're you grinning?"

But Carter doesn't answer. Instead, he reaches into his baggy jeans — the kind most kids wear but I feel funny in — and he pulls something out, but I can't see what.

"Here, old sport. For your trip. A gift. From me to you."

I hold out my hand, just to find out what it is. He drops something small and square into my open palm, and then jumps out of the chair to leave.

"You watch out for those fast Manhattan women. And if you get into a sticky situation — if you know what I mean — just use that and you'll be fine."

I look down to see he's given me a condom: a Trojan Lubricated Ultra-Thin condom with a receptacle tip. I can even see the ringed shape of the rubber through the grey metallic package. I wonder just how long Carter's had this thing. How long has it been hibernating in those jeans? I bet it's gone through the wash half a dozen times.

"What the hell is this for?"

"If you don't know *that*, Perry, my friend," he laughs, "then there truly is no hope for you. Well, I should go."

I try to stop him, but he's gone – in a cloud of giggling – before I can persuade him to take the condom back.

Despite all of my travelling over the years back and forth between various relatives in dozens of states around the country, not to mention the times Mom and I have relocated when she was ending one marriage and on the verge of beginning another, I've only taken the train twice. Other than that, it's just been Mom and me in a rented van, and if the trip was longer than a few hundred miles, we'd just fly. I've only been on a train two times in my life because there was no reason to take it a third or fourth time. I guess I'm just one more of a generation spoiled by air travel.

On Saturday afternoon, my mother insists that we get to the MetroNorth station ridiculously early. She's always been a fanatic about arriving early: for every plane trip I've ever taken with her, we've shown up hours ahead of time. Like today: even though my train's not supposed to leave until three, she made sure we were at the station promptly at two. I'm surprised she didn't make me camp out the night before.

To kill time we go to a little snack bar and, even though I had a big breakfast, I get a muffin and some orange juice and, even though it's hot out, Mom gets a cup of coffee. We find the platform my train will be leaving from and sit down on a set of benches in front of a window which overlooks the rusting train tracks and a set of thick trees on the other side.

For some reason, she's acting awfully nervous and her eyes are red and look on the verge of tears. I figure maybe it's because we haven't spent a day apart in a long time. In fact, for a while there, during those last few weeks in Arizona and during the drive out to New York, she and I spent every second with each other.

Sometimes, the look I see on her face is that she never wants me to leave, yet she knows this has to happen. She knows that one day I'll turn eighteen and college will be just the beginning of the long casting away of my life from hers. After that, it's just the weekly phone call and the occasional visit. I mean, look at Josh: we see him once a year, if we're lucky, and I know that breaks my mom's heart. I know she's afraid of the same thing happening with me, that I'll leave home, go to college some place far away, and never return. I think she'd kidnap me from becoming an adult, if she somehow could.

When the train finally comes, we've been sitting around the station for almost an hour, and I'm glad to end the awkward silence of she and I waiting alone in the cavernous station. She tells me that the trains are only busy on the weekdays, when hundreds of commuters, men and woman in business suits with their cups of coffee and copies of *The Wall Street Journal*, travel between Walther and New York City for their jobs. This sounds crazy to me, sitting on a train for four hours a day just so you can sit at a desk in Manhattan for another nine.

"You be safe, OK? And don't talk to strangers, and don't go out at night alone. Without Josh, I mean. And you listen to whatever he says, all right? He knows the city, so you listen to him. You hear me?"

I'm trying to get on the train but she won't let me. A conductor wearing a blue suit and hat leans out from between trains and keeps looking at his watch. Mom and I are probably derailing their whole schedule. Finally she lets me go, but not until after a bone-crushing bearhug, and when I take a window seat in the next to last car, I can see her standing on the platform beginning to cry. I'm afraid that, when the train starts moving, she's going to run alongside, as if I was her young fiancé going off to war. Thankfully, when the train pulls out of the station my mother just stands there and finally, for the first time in her life, lets me leave without a making a scene.

I settle into my seat, which is actually pretty comfortable, and for the first half-hour I just watch the countryside roll by. It's funny, but every small town we pull through – Patterson, Brewster, Croton Falls – looks just like Walther. Every town has a cluster of similar-looking houses, one or two malls, the usual selection of fast food restaurants, a bank sprinkled here and there, and one of those gigantic movie theatres which show eight or ten films at a time. It used to be that every small town was different, each with its own charm, but now they're all the same. These days, small towns are just part of one big town, a whole damn country which, wherever you go, is exactly the same.

The closer we get to Manhattan, the more passengers we pick up. When I got on in Walther there were only a few other people on the train but now that we're just a half-hour away, almost every seat is occupied. For the first hour I had my backpack sitting in the seat next to me, and every few minutes I'd pick up one of the magazines I brought and try to read a few lines, but now, because the train is filling up, I know that someone's going to end up sitting next to me.

Right after I tuck my backpack under the seat in front of me, a cute red-headed girl, around my age, wanders down the aisle and stops in front of me and says, "Is this seat taken?"

Too nervous to speak, I just nod my head from side to side.

She sits down and, when she does, I can smell the perfume she's wearing. The scent is rosy but also smells a little like powder, like the stuff Mom uses which feels like confectioner's sugar and comes in a round black and yellow box, topped with a soft powder puff.

The girl is wearing a long green dress, but when she crosses her legs I can see that they're very white, almost pale. Her arms and neck are also pale, the skin here and there sprinkled with freckles. That's something I've noticed about redheads: they're almost always pale and have freckles. In fact, I don't think I've ever seen a tanned redhead in my life. I think it's impossible.

"Going to New York City?" the girl asks.

I'm glad she said something, because I never would have had the guts.

"Yes. You, too?"

"Yeah."

"Family?"

She just nods.

"Me too."

"Aunt."

"Brother."

"That's funny."

Like an idiot, I reply, "Yeah, that *is* funny."

In the silence that follows, while she's waiting for me to say words which I'm too nervous to produce, she pulls out of her purse a book covered in paisley fabric. It's just like the blank book Bob gave me, except that I can see that hers is filled with page after page of curly hand-writing. I wonder whether she calls it a *journal* or a *diary*, but I'm too embarrassed to ask.

She places the book on her lap, opening it to a page only half-filled with confession, and then continues to search for something in her purse. After a few minutes, she finally gives up and reluctantly turns back to me.

"I'm sorry, but," she says, pausing to smile. Even

though she wears braces, she has a nice smile. "Do you have a pen? I guess I lost mine."

I'm about to answer "No" when I remember that my mom gave me a pen back at the station after she made me add four more emergency phone numbers to the list of a dozen she already gave me.

"Yeah, actually, I do."

When I reach into my pocket to get it, my hands – out of nervousness – grab the first thing they find and just as I'm ready to give her the pen, I discover that what I've grabbed is the condom. For some reason I brought it, not because I thought I'd get a chance to use it, but because I was afraid my mother would find it if I left it in my room. No matter where you hide something, a parent will always find it (especially something like this). And I didn't want Mom to see it because it would just mean another lecture on sex and responsibility, about how it's OK to wait, blah, blah, blah.

Now this girl's looking at me, wanting something to write with, and what I'm about to hand her is a Trojan Lubricated Ultra-Thin rubber with a receptacle tip.

"Oh, uh, sorry. Hang on, that's my train ticket."

"But I thought they already *took* the tickets."

"Must've skipped me . . . I guess."

I shove my hand back into my pocket, releasing the condom from my sweaty grasp, and then pull out the cheap plastic ballpoint pen my mom gave me back in Walther.

"Here you . . . go."

She takes the pen from me but, from the look on her face, I can see that the pen is all she wants. If she might have been willing to give me a chance a few minutes ago, maybe even giving me the phone number of where she's staying in Manhattan, now she just curls up in her seat, keeping as far away from me as possible.

When we finally pull into Grand Central Station, after crossing a bridge from the Bronx into Manhattan, the girl I'm sitting next to won't even look at me. Instead, when the train comes to a halt, she closes her paisley covered book after writing half a dozen pages (probably about me — about what a jerk I am) and hands back the pen, saying "Thanks" in that polite voice which all parents teach their children.

I want to explain, to maybe salvage the nice moment we had, but I lose her as everyone in the car gets up and begins to retrieve their luggage and bags from beneath seats and overhead compartments. My backpack gets stuck on a foot rest, and by the time I wrench it free the girl is gone, already off the train, and probably halfway to her aunt's apartment where she'll forget all about me.

I put on my backpack and carry my bag down a long sloping ramp which leads to an underground maze of tunnels, signs above which point to the street, subways, and additional train tracks. I look behind me and can see how dozens of sets of tracks sit side by side, where passengers from all over the state are constantly delivered to this tiny island. It's hard to believe that I'm on an island. You expect an island to be tropical, with sand and palm trees, not traffic and skyscrapers.

I follow the signs which say CAB STAND, so I can get a taxi to take me to Josh's. As I'm led through the main area of Grand Central Station, I decide that it's maybe the most beautiful building I've ever been in. If nothing else, it's definitely the biggest. The lobby area (or whatever you want to call it) is almost as big as a football field, with ornately decorated walls and arched windows rising up four or five stories. Painted on the ceiling, against a sea-foam green backdrop, is a mural of all the constellations. Looking up is like looking at the night sky, except that all of the constellations are reversed, so it's like the view God must have whenever He looks down on us – if He ever does.

There are hundreds of people all around me, pushing and shoving their way to get on to trains; or maybe they're like me, just getting off and trying to catch cabs or buses in order to get to wherever they have to go. Everyone's in such a rush, you'd think each person was running their own personal marathon. I've never seen so many people in one spot before; that is, so many people who weren't at a concert or baseball game or something like that. I must have brushed shoulders with dozens of people already, and I just got off the train five minutes ago. Thousands, maybe millions, cross this marble floor every day.

I finally find the cab stand, which consists of a velvet rope behind which are twenty or so people, most of them travellers, like myself, carrying a few pieces of luggage or just a backpack. At the head of the line is a man in uniform – he looks sort of like bellhops look in old movies – and he stands in a little driveway waving cabs in from the street, and opening the doors for the passengers when the taxis finally stop.

As I get closer and closer to the front of the line, I begin to get nervous. From a distance, I can see that the man is talking to each person – he opens the door, says something, and then the person gets in – but from this far back I can't hear what's being said. I figure that he's asking the people where they're going, because maybe some taxis only go downtown, or uptown, or to the airport, or to Jersey or wherever. I start to get a little scared. New York must have millions of rules, and suddenly I think I'm breaking them all. Like a chant I begin reciting Josh's address, to make sure I don't choke up when the old man asks me, sending me to the end of the line or, even worse, back on the train and back to Walther for the week.

Finally, it's my turn. I step up to the head of the line, to a stretch of sidewalk where the velvet rope is attached to a brass pole. The man waves a taxi into the crescent-shaped driveway and then steps off the kerb, his hand outstretched and waiting for the car door to appear in front of him, the way they do all day, hundreds of them. He probably sees taxis in his sleep.

When I finally get a look at him, I see that he's pretty old, with grey hair and pale skin sagging with wrinkles.

The suit – with its flourishes of gold decoration around the cuffs and collar – is too big for him, and he looks almost like a little boy wearing his father's clothes. He opens his mouth to speak and, no matter that he looks like a kindly old grandfather, now I'm sure the interrogation is going to begin.

"Hello, sir. Have a nice day."

That's all he says. He doesn't yell at me or demand to see my passport, it's just "Hello, sir" and "Have a nice day". Before I know it, the door is lightly shut and I'm in the back seat of a yellow car pulling out into the noise and traffic of a bright Manhattan afternoon. I was such an idiot to be scared, to be afraid. I lean forward and tell the driver Josh's address, and suddenly we're on our way; the first potential disaster of my trip has been avoided. I begin to relax when suddenly it hits me. *Shit.* I probably should have given that guy a tip.

You can't see anything from the back seat of a cab in New York City. You can't see anything because the buildings are so tall that you're left in a sort of valley with skyscraper cliffs on either side, and if you look out the window, all you'll see are people walking on the street in front of high-rise buildings which seem to block out the sun.

When my taxi pulls out, I think we're somewhere near the Chrysler Building, but I can't be sure because I can't see the tops of any buildings. I can't see the skyline or any of those famous landmarks, like what's printed on countless postcards or in every other movie. The only way to see anything at all is to look through the dirty glass in front of you, past the shoulder of your driver stuck in traffic, except what's directly in front of you, most of the time, is just another cab with someone in the back seat, who's looking forward into the back of the cab in front of them, etc.

Josh and Kendra live in an apartment in a section of the city called the Upper West Side. It's where a lot of young people and families live, along with a lot of rich people – but not terribly rich people. (The *really* rich live on the Upper East Side, although you've got to have more money than usual just to live anywhere in Manhattan.) The Upper West Side has a reputation for being home for a lot of Yuppies, and I wonder if that's what my brother considers him and his wife these days.

Josh works in public relations and Kendra works in publishing. A few times he's told me how much money both of them make, and either of their salaries is an awful lot, more than I bet our mom has ever made. Every time he's told me, Josh has tried to act all embarrassed about it, as if he didn't really care how much money he makes, but I know that it means a lot to him and that he likes to show it off. He's climbed the first few rungs of the corporate ladder, and he's proud of it. It's hard to believe this is the same guy who used to punch my arm until it turned blue.

For a second I get nervous that maybe the cab driver is taking the long way to Josh's place, just to inflate the fare, because every street we turn down is stuffed with traffic. Half the time we're not even moving, but that doesn't mean the meter doesn't stop ringing up a bill. My luggage and my age must have told him I'm a tourist ripe to be ripped off. I lean forward, to ask him if we're going in the right direction, but he's too busy talking on a cell phone in some language that sounds so strange I can't even tell what it is. I just sit back in the seat, afraid to interrupt.

When we finally get to Josh's block, I pull out my wallet and realize how stupid I had been to think that this guy was trying to scam me. After all, why would he scam a kid? How much money could I possibly have?

As I'm waiting for the light to change so I can cross the street (not that anybody else waits — it's jaywalk city), a short old woman comes up to me and says something very quickly in a vaguely Spanish accent.

Soft of confused, I don't say "Excuse me?" or even the more polite "Pardon?" which Mom taught me. Instead, all I say is, "Huh?"

She repeats what she said before.

"Is today Monday or Sunday?"

"Uh, actually, it's *Sat*urday."

She takes in the information and then continues walking down Broadway. Before I can even begin to think how someone could not know what day it is, the traffic stops behind a red light and I'm swept up in a wave of pedestrians crossing Eighty-Eighth Street.

Their building has a doorman, which means a guy in

a booth in the lobby has to call upstairs to make sure I'm expected. He's also wearing a funny suit that makes him look like a bellhop, just like the guy at the train station, and I'm wondering if this one's going to take my bags for me, or if he's going to want a tip. I just got here and already my money's starting to disappear.

At first I don't see him and just march right through the lobby. I'm halfway to the elevators, which I can see are on the left, opposite a bank of mailboxes, when a rough clearing of the throat designed to attract my attention, does.

"Can I help you, sir?" The doorman is leaning on a sign right inside the large glass doors that reads ALL VISITORS MUST BE ANNOUNCED. I tell him my name, he picks up a phone, and a few seconds later he says, "Go right up, Mr Mathews."

My brother greets me at the elevator, although I don't know why. Does he really think I'm so stupid I'll get lost in the hallway while trying to find apartment 407?

"Per-*ree!*"

Josh envelops me in a bear-hug, lifting me off my feet although this is harder to do than it used to be since I'm now almost as tall as he is.

He stands back to look at me, trying to measure how much I've grown and changed since Christmas. When he does this, it's my chance to examine him.

We definitely look alike. I mean, you can tell we're brothers, but we're certainly not twins or anything like that. My face is longer, like my mom's, while Josh got most of our dad's traits: a little short, sort of stocky, with a rounder face and curlier hair. I wouldn't call my brother very handsome, but he convinced a girl to marry him, so he must be hiding charm somewhere.

"Shit, kid, you've *grown*! What's Mom feeding you that she didn't feed me? I didn't hit six feet till I was a junior in high school. At this rate, you'll be a centre for the Knicks by the time you're a sophomore."

I just sort of laugh as he leads me down the carpeted hallway. The door to his apartment is slightly ajar, and Josh opens it fully with a kick of his foot.

"Oh, *Ken*-dra!" he calls out. "We have a *visi*-tor!"

She steps out from the kitchen, where she must have been washing something because she's still wiping her hands on a washcloth when she enters the long hallway.

Kendra's wearing a floral printed summer dress, which fits snugly over her thin, tanned body. Her blue eyes look brighter in person than they did in the wedding photos, and where her hair was partly obstructed that day due to a lace veil pinned in it, today it's parted down the middle and flowing over her caramel-brown shoulders.

It's hard to believe that this stranger standing in the hallway is my sister-in-law and that I've never met her in person. It's an even stranger thought when I upgrade her looks from Attractive to Beautiful.

There's an awkward couple of seconds when I don't know whether to shake her hand or give her a hug – but just as I'm sticking out my arm, she says, "Oh,

Perry, come here," and she also gulps me up in an embrace.

Her hair feels soft against my face, and I can smell the perfume rising from the back of her neck. The scent is so nice it almost makes me drunk. All these women with all that perfume. If there really is a war of the sexes, it certainly isn't a fair fight.

"How was your trip? Was it OK?"

"Jesus, Kendra," my brother says in a groan, "it was a train ride from upstate, not a twenty-hour flight. I'm sure it was just fine."

"Then why don't you let Perry tell me it was fine? Huh, Josh?"

"It was fine, just fine," I blurt out, hoping to break some of the tension that seems to exist between them. Suddenly I wonder if my coming here was such a great idea, but it's too late to worry about that now.

While Josh shows me around the apartment, I notice Kendra tucking my bags beside a couch in the living-room which will be my bed for the week. It's a nice apartment, but small. The bathroom's tiny and my little crooked bedroom back in Walther is almost as big as Josh and Kendra's. When I tell him this, my brother just laughs and informs me that their apartment is large by New York City standards.

"Hell, we're lucky to have this place. A doormanned apartment on the Upper West Side? Right off Broadway? You know how hard that is to get?"

Before I can reply, "No, Josh, I don't," Kendra

interrupts by saying, "*You* were lucky? I had this apartment when you were still in the dorms figuring out whether or not you wanted to go to grad school."

"Well, sure, but that's because your mom *bought* the place *for* you." Josh turns from his wife and looks at me. He says, "It's true, Perry. All Kendra and I do is cover the mortgage, although it's still a lot, trust me."

Kendra walks by Josh on her way to the back of the apartment, and she slaps him as she passes. It seems to me like less of a love-tap than a real slap. Josh yells out "Hey!" and he's still rubbing the red spot on his arm as he shows me the view on to Broadway.

"Can you believe it, kid? You're here. By way of Seattle, Portland, Tucson and now, what's that shitty little town up there called?"

"Walther," I answer. "With an H in there, although it's silent."

"Yeah, I bet it is. So, you like it up in Walther?"

Josh says Walther like *Wall-ther*, even though I told him not to.

"Things going OK?"

Before I can answer, Kendra calls Josh to the bedroom. After rolling his eyes, as if to say, *What's her problem now?*, he joins her in the bedroom and I can hear them fighting about something. I stick my head out the window, so I hear the traffic instead of their bickering voices.

"OK, kid, change of plans," Josh says when he rejoins me a few minutes later. "We're not going out for pizza, the way I promised."

"But what about what you said? You said my first meal in Manhattan would be that thin, greasy pizza you're always telling me about."

When we spoke on the phone earlier in the week, to firm up the details of my trip, going out for pizza had been one of the few plans we made. The rest was all vague and, with him working during the week, I just sort of figured I'd be on my own most of the time. But not tonight. I was really looking forward to having pizza. Right now, I'm starving for it.

"Sorry, kid. Kendra had it for lunch. I told her not to, but she says she doesn't remember me telling her. Which is bullshit. Anyway, how does Vietnamese sound?"

"What? Food from *where*?"

"Viet*nam*. Listen, I know what you're thinking . . . that we lost the war and all, but come on, kid, have an open mind. You'll *like* it. Trust me. There's a spectacular place down the block."

"What's it called, The Hungry Deer Hunter?"

This makes Josh laugh, but I can tell that his giggles are just covering up a nervousness.

"No, you big joker, it's called Saigon Grill." He turns and shouts back to where Kendra must be getting her purse or something, engaged in one of those female things which always take a long time. "Honey, you should have just heard what Perry said! The Hungry Deer Hunter!"

But she can't hear us, and just yells back, "What?"

Josh, turning back to me, reads the pained looked on my face.

"Come on, kid, just give it a chance. You'll like it, it's just like Chinese food."

"Then why don't we just get Chinese food?"

Josh laughs for a second, but then turns serious.

"Because Kendra can't stand Chinese food. Anyway, don't worry about it. You'll love it."

As we head down the hallway, for my first meal in the city, I ask, "Josh, do *you* love it?"

"No, kid, I don't. But that's not the point."

The next morning, Kendra decides she wants to make waffles. She announces this with an embarrassed look on her face, and for a second I think she's going to admit to something really bad, like that she's pregnant or not in love with my brother any more – two facts I'd probably believe if she told me. But instead, what she's got to tell us both is that she's never made waffles before.

"Oh, hon, why don't you wait and try that next week, when the kid's not here? I don't want you ruining his little vacation with one of your various culinary experiments."

Josh says this without looking at her or even lowering the newspaper he's been reading all morning. His voice from behind the multiple pages of newsprint is muffled and sounds remote. It feels like it's just Kendra and I in the room, with Josh on a speakerphone talking from very far away.

"Next thing you know, she'll try and make curry again."

I'm just about to ask what *curry* is, when Kendra crosses the room and draws down the top of Josh's *New York Times* with the tongue of a wooden spoon.

"Josh, baby, it won't be so bad. Waffles are just square pancakes, and you know what an ace I am at making those."

"Yeah, an ace."

Josh looks at me, winking before he speaks. I recognize the mischievous look on his face, and I can tell that whatever he's about to say will probably make fun of Kendra.

"You should see them, kid. Burnt on the outside and batter on the inside. It's incredible. I don't know how she does it."

So that someone in the room with the last name of Mathews is nice to her this morning, I say, "That's OK, Kendra. I *like* batter."

"Shut up, kid. Pancake batter's not like cake batter, or muffin batter, or raw cookie dough. Pancake batter's horrible. You *can't* eat it. It's bitter and tastes all buttermilky. It's like . . . paste."

Kendra lifts the spoon and the paper automatically rises again in front of Josh's face. As she passes me on her way through the living-room, she bends over and says, "Well, none of that matters anyway, because I'm not making *pan*cakes, I'm making *waf*fles." Since she doesn't deny what Josh said about her pancakes, I figure it's true.

"God, kid, you really should taste them sometime, just as an experiment. I warn you now though, you'll be risking your life if you do."

Josh chuckles to himself and then turns silent, his attention, I guess, sucked back into the story he was reading before Kendra's announcement broke his train of thought.

The mention of cake batter reminds me of the few years that I can remember when Josh lived at home, before he went away to college. I remember him showing me how to guide my pudgy fingers carefully in and out of the two little metal cages of Mom's pea-green hand-held mixer. I can still taste the lemony cake batter we used to divide – one beater each – and how he'd then con Mom into making a little extra chocolate frosting just for us, which she always did. For the rest of the day I'd dip my fingers repeatedly into that bowl of frosting, pausing only to watch her artfully glaze the golden brown cakes using a long, thin knife with a squared tip. On top of the cake she made an intricate crisscross pattern which used to always amaze me; still does.

"Perry, how many of them would you like?"

"What?" I call back, distracted by everything going on around me: Josh, Kendra, the noise of Manhattan outside their window.

"Why, waffles, dear. How many would you like?"

"Really, Kendra, don't do that. Let's take the kid out, for Christ's sake. It's his first day. You've got all week to punish him."

"We will take him out, for dinner. But right now, I want to make waffles."

"But you don't know *how*."

"Will you let me at least *try*? I mean, I just bought the wafflemaker yesterday. Give me a chance."

"I know, and you *will* try, just later, when you're not using my brother as a goddamn guinea pig."

"I'm sure Perry doesn't mind –"

"Perry's too polite to say anything, aren't you, kid?"

My brother quickly looks at me, but doesn't leave me any time to respond. He just goes back to yelling across the room at Kendra.

"Besides, it's hot enough in here already. I don't want that griddle-thingy, or whatever it is, steaming up the place even more. I mean, who cooks in the summer? This whole place feels like an oven as it is."

This time, my brother's right. Outside it's hot and humid, and the apartment is old and was built before air-conditioning. They've got a unit in the bedroom, which Kendra put in a few years ago, but it cools just the bedroom and nothing else. The air-conditioner is a rectangular metal box which fits halfway in the window and sticks halfway out, and whenever it's on it sounds like an old photocopier constantly making copies. In the kitchen and the living-room there are two rotating fans, but all those do is throw the hot air right back at you.

"Silly," Kendra calls out, "it's not a *griddle*, it's a *waffle*maker. And it's not just *any* wafflemaker, it's a Krups."

Just as I'm about to ask what a *krups* is, Josh tosses the paper to the ground and storms across the room, rounding the corner into the kitchen so quickly that his socks slip on the tile floor. None of my questions are being answered because, between the two of them shouting back and forth, I haven't had the time even to ask.

After a minute of arguing as quietly as they can — which is still pretty loud — Josh walks back into the living-room. But this time he moves slowly, with hunched shoulders. He's almost crawling.

Sitting down on the couch, he picks up the *Times* from where it landed in an angular heap on the floor. He puts it back in front of his face.

After a few seconds of silence tensely roll by, I ask, "So, we going out?"

"No." His voice is muffled again and sounds far away. "We're having waffles."

In the kitchen, Kendra proudly shows off her new appliance. Josh's out getting some bagels and orange juice, and I can tell that Kendra's glad to have him gone, if just for a few minutes so she can tell me about her new wafflemaker without him making fun of her from the other room. She says she bought it the day before on a whim at a store on Broadway called Lechters. She keeps telling me that she doesn't know why she bought it, she just did.

"Really, Perry, I only went in there to buy a couple of these plastic picture frames. Buying something like *this* was the last thing on my mind. But they were having this amazing sale so I thought, what the hell." She puts a blue box of waffle mix on the counter and leans into me and begins to whisper, which doesn't make sense since Josh's still not back. "To be honest, I don't even remember if I *like* waffles. I mean, it's been years since I had them."

Now that she mentions this, it strikes me that it's been a long time since I've had waffles myself, and when I did, they were just the frozen kind you heat up in the toaster. I remember them tasting like nothing special, if anything, they were always sort of stale. The best part was how I'd always smear butter on the top, making sure every little square was filled.

"But these aren't regular waffles, so don't worry about it."

"What kind of waffles are they?"

A large smile grows on her face when she tells me.

"Belgian!" she announces.

I seem to remember having Belgian waffles once before. They're bigger than regular waffles, with fewer squares on top; a normal waffle might have a dozen while Belgian waffles only have four or six. That won't make my spreading butter in each one as much fun, but I don't tell Kendra this.

Trying to keep up her enthusiasm, I say, "Wow, Belgian waffles. I don't think I've ever had those before."

"Oh, I'm sure you have, Perry. *Every*body's had

Belgian waffles. I mean, *please*." After she says this she turns away, to the cabinet, but then turns back and shoots me an embarrassed look, like maybe I haven't had Belgian waffles before, and maybe I'm just not as sophisticated as she thought.

Josh has told me before about how Kendra was raised in a rich suburb just outside of Columbus. In fact, in the living-room, above the mantel, there's a picture made out of needlepoint of a big house that I'd almost call a mansion. When I first saw it, I asked Josh if the building was a museum and he said, "No, that's where Kendra grew up. Can you believe it? Some *servant* made that for Kendra's mom, but the old bag hated it, so she gave it to Kendra. Nice, huh?" But the tone in my brother's voice at the time seemed to imply that it wasn't so unbelievable that a maid had stitched a portrait of a home in needlepoint, but what was unbelievable was that he was married to the woman whose home that used to be. I always thought my big brother was made of nothing but confidence, like most little brothers do, but now I'm starting to think that's not the case.

"Anyway, Perry, I hope you'll help me make them."

"What? The waffles? Oh, sure."

Kendra takes from the cabinet a bottle of seltzer water and hands it to me along with a measuring cup. She tells me to mix two cups of the water with a heap of waffle mix she's already measured into a bowl.

"You know, Josh's right about my pancakes. They *are* horrible. Burnt and raw at the same time. Really. I even set off the smoke detector once." She points at the ceiling with the wooden spoon, to a round circle of plastic with a blinking red light in the centre. "I like to cook, really, I do. The problem is, I'm just not *good* at it. I never had anyone to teach me how to cook when I was growing up. My mom, even *she* didn't cook. We always had, you know, someone to cook *for* us. So I never got a chance to learn how to do these things for myself. *Any*thing. I never even did my own laundry until I was twenty-four, till after I got out of college. Leftovers I'm a whiz at, but stuff from scratch, forget it."

As she tells me about her privileged past, the needlepoint portrait above the mantel comes to life in my mind, and I can see Kendra as a little stitch-girl being attended to by a faceless servant made out of black thread. I begin to realize why my brother's always so defensive around her and quick to criticize. It's as if, with every smart alecky comment, he's showing Kendra that he's just as good as she is, that he's just as smart and his head is as full with as many ideas. Hell, my brother barely graduated from college. I know that must keep him up at night when sleeping next to a girl like Kendra, who went to a place called Brown (and any college named after so dull a colour is probably pretty good).

"Now, Perry, watch the seltzer water because sometimes —"

But before Kendra can finish her sentence, I unscrew the top of the bottle and instantly there's a burst of spray and then the water begins to gush out as if it were a garden hose turned on full blast. I try to replace the lid but it's too late; the water quickly escapes, flying in every direction. By the time the geyser dies down, most of the kitchen – the cabinets, the sink, the countertop, even Kendra and I – are splattered with sparkling water. Paralyzed with embarrassment, I just stand there, dripping wet, staring at a puddle which has started to form on the floor beneath me.

"That's OK," Kendra quietly says. "It's happened to me before, believe me. The bottles get shaken up sometimes, you know, coming home from the store or something. Don't worry about it. Really, I've done it before, too."

I know she's trying to make me believe none of this is my fault, but it's not working. I feel like a complete idiot. If I could disappear, I would. I feel just like I did last month standing in Gus's Diner with Carter and Donna staring at me – each of them wanting me to say the right thing. I thought I was going to die from a heart attack then, and it's how I feel right now. If this happens to me one more time this summer, I just might not make it to next summer.

"Honestly, Perry, it's no problem." From my hands she takes the large bottle, which is now almost empty since most of its contents are soaked into the kitchen and our clothes. "You know, it's *my* fault. I should have just used tap water. The box says you can use tap water, but I was just trying to be fancy."

"Kendra, stop. It's not your fault, it's *mine*. I'm a

clumsy idiot. I'm always doing stupid things like this, trust me."

I feel Kendra's hand under my chin, which raises my face to hers. She looks at me right in the eyes.

"Don't say that, Perry. You're *not* stupid. It was an accident, OK? They happen. All right?" She says all this without blinking, her eyes trained on my own which are quickly fluttering open-and-closed like humming-bird's wings. "Listen, you'd better go put on a new T-shirt before Josh comes home. Maybe I can clean this up so he won't notice. The last thing I need from him this morning is an 'I told you so'."

As I turn to leave the kitchen, I look back and can see that her T-shirt is also pretty wet. Underneath the white cotton front, which has been turned slightly transparent due to the soaking, I can see the ornate lace pattern of her bra which covers her breasts in two crescents. Gulping, I quickly grab a T-shirt from my suitcase in the living-room and retreat to the bathroom. While I'm in there, trying like hell to forget the image of Kendra in her bra, Josh returns.

Through the locked bathroom door I can hear him drop off a small bag of groceries, toss a ring of keys on to the table, and then enter the kitchen. As I'm reaching for a handful of Kleenex, I hear his voice shout out, "What the hell happened to *you*?"

Despite all of the tension from earlier in the day, break-fast turned into the casual, easygoing affair that Kendra,

Josh and myself had hoped it would be. Even after my mistake with the seltzer, Kendra allowed me back into the kitchen to help. I also think this was because Josh instantly resumed his position on the couch, with the paper in front of his face, and the meal was turning into quite a production for a girl who was used to just leftovers.

I was in charge of pouring the batter into the waffle-maker. The appliance was pretty small – it only made two waffles at a time – and had a black handle and a shiny silver top. It looked like a toaster resting on its side. The inside was made out of a black metal that Kendra told me was so slick we didn't even need to use butter or shortening (that was another thing she hated about pancakes: they were always sticking to the pan). She also told me that the waffles were fat free, so was the syrup, and that we shouldn't feel bad for having something so sweet so early in the morning because it really wasn't as bad as it seemed. "Doughnuts," she told me, "now *those* are killers."

When I made the first couple of waffles, I was afraid to pour in too much batter (which would have caused it to run off the side, on to the counter, making another big mess), so I scooped out just a little. When I raised the lid after five minutes, I discovered that the waffles were thin, with sort of tattered edges, and weren't even full squares. Josh took one look at them and chuckled silently to himself, and I could tell he was on the verge of delivering an "I told you so", but he restrained out of some sort of sentimental mercy for either Kendra or myself, or maybe it was just the pitiful sight of both of us combined that made him resist.

The next two batches, however, came out perfect: golden brown, light and fluffy, with each of the squares on top deep and perfectly formed. The wafflemaker really worked well, and didn't make the kitchen any hotter than it already was, like Josh complained it would. In fact, I didn't even have to pry the waffles out with the wooden spoon Kendra gave me (she said that a metal one would scratch the surface). Instead, I just grabbed the hot edges with my hands and quickly tossed them on to a plate. Rather than think this was sanitarily questionable, Kendra was impressed by my skill. I'd learned it from my stepdad in Arizona; that's the way he used to flip tortillas.

By the time we all sat down to eat, the waffles had turned a little chewy (something Kendra heard might happen if they were left out in the air too long before eating), but other than that they were delicious. The taste reminded me of thick, soggy ice cream cones.

For syrup Kendra had bought authentic maple syrup from Vermont. I looked at the price tag when she placed it on the table, and just about died because it cost over ten dollars. It didn't even come in a squeezable bottle, like most brands, but instead came in a metal container, like turpentine you'd buy at the hardware store. Also, it didn't have a plastic flip-up lid; instead there was a metal cap that screwed on and off like on a gas tank. It was about the fanciest syrup I'd ever seen, even though it wasn't the best I'd ever tasted. It was thin and watery and tasted almost bitter, but this made sense seeing how it was drained straight from a tree into the little flask-like can which sat in the middle of the table. For ten bucks you would think they could add some sugar and make it a little thicker.

Even though I didn't like the syrup, the bagels Josh bought were about the best I'd ever had in my life. They were so good, he said, because they were fresh. When he brought them home, they were still warm. To go on the bagels, Josh brought out some French jam he told me he'd ordered out of a catalogue and which cost eight dollars. (I didn't know which to be more astonished at, the price or the fact that he'd ordered jam out of a catalogue. I tried to guess whether our mom would be proud of him, or think he was as crazy as I did.) The white label on the small jar read *La Trinquelinette*, which I tried to pronounce, giving up after the second syllable of my horrible and clichéd French accent. Kendra laughed when I did this, but Josh just told me to shut up, and that I wasn't classy enough for his jam. Then *I* laughed, because I remembered that when we were growing up he'd eat anything you'd shove in front of him – he was a regular junk food junkie – and now he was trying to act like this big gourmet in front of his wife.

Instead of reminding him of his embarrassing past, I kept quiet and just ate my bagel. The jam was definitely good, but I couldn't tell that it was that much better than what Mom buys for me at our regular grocery store, which comes from America and costs maybe two or three bucks instead of eight. I figured that what Josh was really paying for was that little white label with the hard to pronounce name. If it wasn't foreign, he wouldn't have bought it.

Looking across the table, I couldn't help but notice what a fancy meal this casual breakfast had turned into: Belgian waffles, French jam, maple syrup from Vermont. Everything seemed to be either imported or expensive, or both. Josh had even bought a tub of cantaloupe chunks from a store called Gourmet Garage, and he carefully arranged a pile on each of our plates. He said that the lightness of the fruit would go well with the heaviness of the waffles. He was right – it made the meal almost perfect.

Even the fruit turned out to be some of the best I'd ever eaten – each piece was soft and sweet, perfectly ripe and without any rind at all. And the orange juice he brought home wasn't a store-bought brand in one of those milk-like containers, but instead he picked up two pints of freshly squeezed juice at a farmer's market on Seventy-Second Street. The juice was delicious: thick, frothy, swimming with chunks of pulp. After breakfast, when I was helping clear the dishes, I told him how much I had enjoyed the meal and how impressed I was. He just tousled my hair and said, "Nothing but the best."

It was a hell of a life my brother was leading. I

wondered if he and Kendra lived and ate like this every day, and something in their nonchalance of everything around them led me to believe that they did. I began to see why he was so intimidated by Kendra. All of this seemed to come so natural to her, but it was all Josh could do to just keep up.

Earlier, when I had given up on pronouncing the name of the jam, and after Kendra stopped giggling because of my attempt, she easily spat out the long foreign word with perfect pronunciation and a convincing accent. If she does not speak French fluently, I'm sure she's been to France several times. After that I became a little nervous around her, as if she were watching my every move and silently judging me against what she had been like when she was fourteen. She seemed too nice to hold my background against me, but still, someone with that much breeding can't help but spot the unenviable traces of a mutt in others.

After I helped Kendra clean the kitchen and do the dishes, and Josh had finished reading the gigantic Sunday edition of the *New York Times*, which was as thick as a phone book, the two of them went for a walk and left me alone in the apartment.

Outside, on Eighty-Eighth Street, someone was repeatedly honking their horn, and the high-pitched squeal of the buses stopping at the corner made it almost impossible to think. In the distance, I counted four different car alarms going off at once, but no one seemed to care; they'd been screaming for a half-hour but police hadn't arrived and pedestrians just walked on by. I don't know how I ever fell asleep last night, but I did.

Sitting in that unfamiliar apartment sent chills down my spine, and I wondered where I was. It's a feeling I've had often during the last couple of months, and just when I thought I had cured myself from feeling it again, here it was, worse than ever. I started to panic, but then I remembered Josh and Kendra, and I calmed down a little. But because I see him so rarely, my own brother seemed to me kind of a stranger, and I still felt uncomfortable being in his apartment when he wasn't around. I still felt like an intruder.

Then the strangest thing happened. I began to miss the odd shape of my room back in Walther. Suddenly, I was homesick for Sis's dusty old house and my little crevice under the stairs. I wanted to be back there, sitting on the bed, staring into that blank book Bob gave me. My throat became wet just thinking of it all, and knowing I'd be back there in a week calmed me enough to be able to make it through the next hour until my brother returned. I didn't think the day would come when I would wish more than anything to be back in Walther, but that's exactly what happened.

Feeling like a tangled-up knot of emotions, and wanting to talk to someone about it, I tried calling Donna. This time, someone answered. At first I was so shocked to hear a human's voice after getting that machine over and over again that it took me a few seconds to figure out what to do.

Finally, I said, "Uh, yeah. Hi. Is, uh, Donna there?"

"No, I'm . . . sorry. She's not." Even though the voice belonged to a female, it wasn't Donna; it was probably her mom.

"Oh, OK. Will she be around later?"

"No, she's out. She'll be out for . . . a while." She said this with a sort of hesitancy which made me believe what she was saying wasn't true. Or maybe I just was being paranoid.

"Well, can I try again tonight?"

There was silence for a second, and I would have thought that maybe the woman hung up except I could hear something in the background: rustling or whispers. Whatever it was, my imagination had a field day picturing the entire family dancing around silently in their socks, laughing without noise and making fun of me.

"She'll be gone tonight . . . too." In the gap between the woman's words, she swallowed deeply, and the *gulp* her action made sounded like a word itself. I'd never seen this person before, and yet I could practically hear her face curling up in embarrassment. The sad, bewildered tone in her voice led me to believe that she always knew that having a daughter would be difficult, but that she never thought it'd be this difficult. Mrs Early thought she was done lying to boys twenty years ago.

"OK, then. Just tell her . . . I mean, don't bother. I mean, nothing."

And with that I hung up the phone.

* * *

For the next week I discovered New York in all the ways that my youth and monetary situation would allow, which meant that I walked everywhere and basically just looked at things.

I couldn't afford to go to a Broadway show, so instead I walked around all of the theatres, taking pictures of the marquees which were brilliantly lit up and flashing on and off, like the casinos of Las Vegas.

I explored around Times Square, which wasn't as seedy or dirty as I'd been led to believe. To be honest, I was a little disappointed. I expected nothing but sex shops and hookers. I expected to be taking my life in my hands if I even entered the area, but instead it was nothing but cheap electronics stores and dozens of guys selling T-shirts (three for ten dollars). All of the pornographic theatres now show regular movies, and the strip clubs have been turned into family restaurants. Josh told me later that Disney came in a few years ago and cleaned up the place, and that most New Yorkers missed the way it used to be.

One afternoon I went downtown to Washington Square and walked around the East and West Village which – with all of the coffee houses, book and record stores, and punk rockers begging for change – reminded me a little of both Portland and Seattle.

A couple of days I walked through Central Park, and each time was really amazing. Everywhere you looked there were joggers and rollerbladers, while men and women were on the Great Lawn playing baseball or were in the Sheep Meadow getting a tan on a huge field of grass surrounded on all sides by skyscrapers. I took a hike on a small trail and almost got lost, losing my way for about half an hour before I popped out behind the Metropolitan Museum of Art. I couldn't believe that, in one of the biggest cities in the world, here I was wiping dirt off my shorts and mud from my shoes. At one point, I was so deep into the trees and bushes that I could no longer hear traffic or sirens or anything, and I didn't feel like I was in New York at all.

Halfway through the week, Manhattan was hit with a heat wave, so I tried to spend as little time as possible in Josh and Kendra's un-air-conditioned apartment. Every morning when I woke up, I left a stain of sweat on their couch which looked like a chalk outline of a murdered body. Every night when I went to bed, even though I was just wearing my boxer shorts and covering myself with a thin sheet, I could barely sleep because of the heat.

Kendra was always the second one to leave the house, Josh disappearing before I was even awake. She didn't seem to mind finding me half-naked on her couch every day, but it sure made me uncomfortable. A few mornings we had bagels and juice and talked in the pleasant shade of the slightly cool kitchen, but other than that I tried to stay out of the apartment as much as I could, heading out for the day before she emerged from the bathroom in just a towel with her wet hair pinned up.

I didn't want Kendra to think I was a burden, or a freeloader, or even that – just because I was Josh's brother – I was always on his side. I had witnessed a few more fights between them, and the next morning Kendra always came to me wanting to know who I thought was right or wrong. This seemed to me like a no-win situation, so I just kept my mouth shut.

One morning she stopped me just as I was about to leave and head out into the bright hot day. I already had the subway token in my sweaty palm when I heard her voice whisper behind me, "Perry?" I thought she was going to offer me food, and if so I had the perfect excuse not to sit and talk with her: "Kendra, sorry, but I'm saving myself for a hotdog and slice of pizza." But she said she wasn't hungry; that it wasn't about that. She just wanted to talk.

After we sat down on the couch, there was nothing in the room but she and I and silence. I decided to let her start the conversation; after all, it had been her idea.

"Has your brother always been like this?" she asked slowly.

"Well, he's at work right now, so I'm not sure what he's like, I mean, right now, and well—"

She cut me off and said, "No, I mean, the temper. The yelling."

The night before, after I'd gone to bed, I heard them having a fight. It lasted for about twenty minutes and for a while I'm sure that half the building could hear them because they were completely shouting at each other. At one point I could hear Kendra crying, and after that Josh said the word "Marriage" and then started laughing like mad. Part of the conversation I could make out clearly even though their door was closed and by then they were whispering: Kendra asked him why they couldn't have a baby. This seemed crazy to me, to want to have a kid with someone you fight with all of the time, but maybe Kendra thought a child would cure some of the problems between them, would make things better even though right now things seemed pretty screwed up. People do that all the time, have a baby to make a marriage work, and then for ever after they put the kid between them like a shield. But that seems pretty selfish. Besides, half the time it doesn't work; that's what my parents did with me, and they got divorced anyway.

"Oh, you mean . . . growing up was he a jerk?"

Kendra just nodded her head.

"Jeez, I don't know what to tell you. I'm not sure what he's said, but we never spent much time together when we were young, what with our age difference. I barely remember . . . I mean, I think of myself most of the time as an only child who somehow has a brother."

This made her laugh, and that made me glad. I couldn't repay her hospitality over the past week with money, but I thought if I at least made her happy once or twice I might almost earn my keep.

"But if you want to know about our home life, yeah, it was rough."

After I said this, I looked away from her. I was ashamed of where I'd come from; all of that fighting and the constant earthquakes between my mom and dad.

And as I turned my head to get away from my past, my eyes instantly settled upon Kendra's past: I was staring right at the framed needlepoint picture of that huge house she grew up in. Suddenly I felt that it was all so simple. *She's got to know that neither of the Mathews boys should be allowed to spend any time with her. We're simply not good enough. Why did she let me into her apartment? Or my brother into her pants?*

"I mean, it's nothing you'd probably understand. It's just, our upbringing wasn't very storybook. I don't mean to say it was a horror novel, either –"

She laughed again.

"– but it was . . . confusing. My dad was barely around and, even when he was, he didn't teach us how to act, you know? And that's what parents do. Or *should* do, anyway, because how else do you learn anything? And you get different things from each one, I think. Well, since my dad was never around when I was growing up my mom's had to perform double duty, trying to teach us everything that's out there. Except she didn't get much of a chance because she had to work all the time, so lots of things fell through the cracks, I guess. Especially, for me, lately." For some reason I stopped speaking and my hand dropped and brushed over my front pocket, and I could feel through the layer of my jeans Carter's condom. "Anyway, I guess Josh's sketchy on a few subjects, too. And one of them is how to treat you."

After I said this, I thought she was going to laugh again, but instead she started to cry. But before she could really get going, I made an excuse that I was late for something (even though this city was so huge it didn't even know I was there), and I got out of the apartment as fast as I could.

On one of the best days of my trip, I took a walk in Riverside Park, which is a long stretch of sidewalks and bike paths winding up the west side of Manhattan and overlooking the Hudson River. I started out at Seventy-Second Street and headed north, back to the apartment after another long and hot day of walking around. It was getting late, already past eight, and the sun was just finishing up its daily escape behind the horizon.

I could see a bridge to the north which connected New York to, I think, New Jersey. I'm pretty sure it was the George Washington Bridge, which Josh told me was around here somewhere. There were yellow lights on the flat part of the bridge with pale blue lights on the curving cables which suspend the bridge below. I looked but, at that distance, couldn't see the head- or taillights of the cars crossing the bridge. I guess I was too far away.

Even though the sun was completely down by that time, it was still light out, the sky coloured a soft lilacky purple, while wide clouds which looked like stretched-out cotton balls were lit up on their bellies orange and pink, but dark purple on top.

Small boats, with their sails down and anchored in the Hudson every fifteen metres or so, were tossed lightly back and forth by the choppy waves, the pointed tips of the water looking like a thousand shark fins. In between two boats a kayaker fought against the current, staying in one place even though his arms rotated wildly, like windmills; no matter how hard he tried, he wasn't going anywhere.

It was nine o'clock before I made it back to the apartment, which of course pissed Josh off. He said that he had made plans for the three of us and that my being late had messed everything up. When I asked him what the plans were, he just dropped the whole subject. Kendra sat there, looking upset, but didn't say anything. It was Friday and I was leaving on Sunday. The minutes left of my trip were ticking by, and I couldn't wait to leave.

On my last day in New York, Josh seems intent on celebrating. I don't know why. I'm not sure exactly what is being celebrated. Maybe he's glad to be getting rid of me, or maybe he had another fight with Kendra and just wants to get out of the stuffy apartment. But for whatever reason, all day he's taken me around Manhattan, buying me slices of pizza or hot dogs and pretzels from those vendors who hang out on almost every street corner. I've spent more time with him today than I have all week. Now it's eleven o'clock at night – we've been at it since ten this morning – and he wants to keep going.

"Go?" I ask. "Go where?"

"A little bar. Downtown. You'll love it. It's on Perry Street. Isn't that great? *Perry* Street."

"Yeah, Josh, thanks for pointing that out to me. *Perry* Street. Yeah, that's also *my* name. Neat. But why now? I'm tired." I lean back on the couch and take off my sneakers. My socks are wet from sweat, from walking around all day. "Besides, a bar? I'm only fourteen. I'm too young even for a fake ID. You don't get those until it's at least *plausible* that you're over twenty-one."

"Oh, it's not really a bar. It's just a little neighbourhood hangout. Only the locals know about it, and they won't bother us. I know the bartender — he'll get us in."

Noticing the worried look on my face, he adds, "Jesus, kid, they only serve wine and beer. OK? Wine and beer . . . that's no big deal. Even *you* can handle that."

It sounds like there's an insult in there somewhere, as if Josh has a whole list of things I can't handle, but I just let the comment slide.

"Listen, where's Kendra? What does *she* have to say about this? Maybe she wants to stay home, too."

"I don't give a shit about Kendra," Josh yells.

He stands up quickly, then sits down, then stands up again — as if there were strings attached to him and someone, somewhere, was jerking him around.

"Kendra's . . . out. I don't *know* where she is. But it doesn't matter. *We* are going downtown to have some fun, OK, little Mr Smarty-pants?"

Now I'm no longer tired, I'm pissed off. My weariness from the day's sightseeing is replaced by seething anger.

"Put your goddamn shoes on, Perry. We're going out."

"Josh, no . . . I'm tired. Can't we just—"

"Shut up and do it." He turns and looks at me, his eyes bloodshot, his chest pumping up and down with excited breaths. *"Now."*

We don't speak for the entire subway ride downtown. He tries to start a conversation now and then, pointing to a crippled homeless man with no arms, or a fat old woman playing a classical guitar at one of the subway stations, but every time he speaks I just ignore him. I'm not really mad any more, I've calmed down from our argument, but I keep acting cold just so he knows how mad I *was*. After all, I can't let him know that I'm easy to push around, or else he'll make a habit of it.

We get off the train in the West Village, which is made up of small streets which intersect at odd angles, unlike the tightly plotted, grid-like symmetry of the rest of the city.

"You should see Wall Street," Josh says as he walks down a dizzying array of side-streets, so many that – even though we just left the subway station – I'm already lost and couldn't find my way back if I had to. "Down there they've got cobblestone streets that are older than the Civil War. Hell, older than America. Back then, the Dutch ruled this city. New Amsterdam, they called it. Then the English. Then, uh, the Dutch again, I think."

I look at the corner street sign he's now pointing at. In white letters on green metal is the word PERRY, just like how I spell my own name. If I were still mad at Josh, even though I'm not, seeing this would have finally smoothed things out for good. It really is pretty cool.

"Wow, that's great. When did you find this?"

Josh crosses the street and wraps himself around the pole, letting his body sag at an angle.

"Maybe a year ago. Maybe two. Actually, I didn't know about this street until someone told me to meet them at the place we're going to tonight. It was, you know, a girl. Like a . . . date. She said the street name and I just cracked up, because of you."

Now I cross the street and look at the sign from close up.

"Perry," I say out loud, for no reason except to give voice to the word that's running through my head.

"Perry," my brother repeats.

He swings himself around the pole a couple of times, and when he comes to a stop he's facing away from me. I can see how he's sweated right through his tan shirt, leaving a dark mark on his back in the shape of a tombstone. This amazes me because, even though it was hot today, it's pretty cool right now. He even changed before we came.

I guess he's just stressed out. I figure that it's all got to do with Kendra, or maybe with that girl he just mentioned, the one he met down here a few years ago. I know that before they got married, he and Kendra dated on and off for almost two years, and I bet the date with this other woman happened during one of the *off* periods. I'm beginning to think it's the things you do when you're not with someone that hurt more than the things you do when you're with them.

"Come on." He releases himself from the pole's grasp, pulling himself away as if it were a magnet and he were a piece of metal. "I need a drink. Let's go."

The bar is called The Other Room, which Josh tells me is because there's another bar a few blocks away which is exactly the same but is named just The Room. I have a feeling he's telling me this in order to hide my face as we enter, which he does with exaggerated hand motions. Once we're inside, he pushes towards the back, and then shoves me down on to a velvet-covered bench in the corner of a small room behind the bar. Josh tells me to stay put and not to talk to anyone while he gets us some drinks.

The room's about half-filled with men and women, some sitting down, some standing, all of them drinking and most of them smoking. Because it's so dark, and there's so much smoke in the air, it's hard to see anybody's face, so no one really pays much attention to me.

Josh was right, it's a small bar – nothing fancy – and there can't be more than fifteen or twenty people in the entire place. Most of them are drinking beer from long, thin glasses rather than bottles. I guess that this bar specializes in microbreweries. When I lived in Portland, that's all I used to hear about: microbreweries. My step-dad back then even used to let me have a beer every once in a while. Even though I hated the taste I still drank it.

My brother rejoins me in the corner, looking both ways before handing me a heavy glass of amber coloured beer. *Ale* they probably call it. I take a sip and discover it's not too bad; almost sweet. Nowadays they mix all sort of things into beer.

"See, what did I tell you? No problem. Just a couple of guys having a brewski." He takes a sip of his own, and has a hard time swallowing with the large grin on his face. He's very impressed with himself.

"Yeah, Josh. Fantastic. Nothing like breaking a few laws to have a little fun."

"Now *that*'s the attitude I want to hear."

I laugh and take another sip, and then I realize he's serious.

"So, little man, I can't believe the whole week's already gone. It went by so *fast*."

I realize Josh is again entering Smalltalk Mode. But this time I humour him, playing along with a few of his lame conversations on boring topics such as the weather and our president who's in trouble yet again because of his personal life. As we talk, I notice my brother is sweating profusely, just like he was on the subway and on the street, except it's even cooler in here than it is outside. In fact, we're sitting right beneath an air conditioner which drenches us in cold air, blowing back the hair on my forehead. But Josh's still sweating. Something's really wrong with him. I think he might be sick, but it seems that the only medicine he'll give himself is more alcohol.

A little later he says "Exchoose me," beginning to slur his speech. He drank five beers in an hour, and now he's beginning to show the effects. "Gotta go to the baffroom."

When I get up in order to let him by, I realize that I'm pretty drunk myself. I only had three beers to Josh's five, but I'm much thinner than he is and dinner was hours ago. When we started drinking I was getting hungry again, and beer is the only thing I've fed that hunger since.

I glance at my watch and discover it's past one. Waiting for Josh to return, I finish the last of my drink just because I'm bored and have nothing else to do.

When I look at my watch again, it's almost two. Now the bar is really crowded, packed even, and I'm staring into all of these strange faces, none of which belong to my brother. I get up and stumble forward in a drunken haze, trying to find the bathroom, except I fall into the backs of three guys leaning against the wall. They all turn to look at me, and one shoves me away with an out-stretched arm, which causes the other two to laugh.

"Sorry," I mumble, though I doubt they can hear me over the music being played, or that I even managed to say the word coherently since I'm pretty drunk and lucky to be standing up at all.

"Josh?" I say out loud as I wander through the crowd, leaning on the wall for support. I bump into the pay phone, knocking the receiver out of its cradle, except I don't put it back. I just keep going and when I turn around I see that the handset is swinging back and forth like the pendulum in a grandfather clock.

"Josh!" I say again, this time almost shouting. The bartender, who's been trained to keep an eye out for trouble, hears me above the music in the background, and his eyes meet mine for a moment. His are filled with suspicion, and mine must be filled with fear. I step backwards, pushing against the bathroom door and stumbling inside.

"Josh. . ."

This time I find him.

My brother is standing in front of the sink, his right hand balled up in a fist and raised to his chin. In his left hand is a small baggy filled with white powder, which he sprinkles on to the back of his other hand. Then, in a quick motion, he plugs one nostril with his free hand and quickly inhales. The powder is instantly vacuumed off his skin. I can't fucking believe this.

I turn to leave, groping for the door.

"Perry, man, wait. Kid," his words come quick, and his voice is start-stop, agitated. "No, man, don't . . . go . . . stay, kid. Perry. Man. *Try* this."

Josh tries to stop me, but with only one of his hands since the other one is still making a fist, ready for the next hit. This tells me all I need to know: he'd rather have the drug than me. I shove open the bathroom door as my head's about to explode out of twelve different forms of anger. I'm pissed off that he dragged me all the way down here just so he could do this, that he didn't tell me anything about it, and that he was going to leave me alone in that corner all night.

Somehow I make it past the bartender, and even the guy at the door checking for IDs, although he never asked me for mine. Suddenly I'm out of the bar, and back on the street. I have no idea where I am. I've taken two steps off the kerb, and already I'm lost.

I look in one direction, down where Perry Street sort of slopes, and I can see water. The river – one of them at least – probably the Hudson. The waves look purple under the vague lighting of the street lamps and cover of night. I don't remember seeing water before, when we approached earlier in the night, so I head in the other direction.

As I walk, zigzagging over the street bumpy with pot-holes, I drunkenly giggle to myself, thinking, *Perry Street*. I notice I'm drooling all over my shirt, so I close my mouth. I try to be serious and figure out how to get home when suddenly I'm hit with a burst of inspiration, what I hear the artists of this world call an *epiphany*: I realize, I'm screwed.

"Hey, you lost?"

A voice comes from out of the shadows and, needing a friend, I gravitate towards it. Getting a little closer, I can see that there are two guys standing in a crevice behind the stone steps of an apartment building. The space reminds me of my room in Walther, which feels a million miles away right now. I start laughing again, thinking, *Walther*.

"Yeah, I'm . . . lost," I say, trying to act as sober as possible. You would have thought these guys were my parents for as much effort as I put into the performance.

"Well then, let me just check my map," the voice says, which causes both of them to break out in laughter. In the darkness, one of them elbows the other and this seems like the signal to start whatever it is they've been waiting here in the shadows to start.

Suddenly a hand comes at me from the sidewalk and lands – knuckles first – on the right side of my face. I'm knocked instantly to the ground and for a second, with my whole head throbbing, I think that I've been hit by a car or something. I can't believe that all of that power could be contained in just one punch. I look around, to see if there are any other survivors from the crash, but all I see are the shrouded images of those two guys, who are still laughing.

I try to get up but am knocked back to the ground, this time by a blow to the other side of my face. Now my whole head is on fire, and I can feel blood trickling down my neck from a cut on my left cheek. I try to get up again, but this time I feel a heavy boot land in the centre of my chest. This drops me to the ground for a third time, where I flip over on to my back like a dying cockroach. I clutch at my stomach and chest, trying to contain the pain. Then I feel more kicks to my side, both of them now joining in, but this doesn't make sense because I'm not going anywhere. I'm already down.

"Stop it, goddamnit!" I want to shout, except the

wind's been knocked out of me, and every time I try to suck in a breath they knock it right back out.

One of them clenches his fists together and heaves his knotted flesh into my bloated stomach, which causes all the beer I drank and what's left of my dinner to explode out of my mouth. The food, almost-digested pizza, sits in a ring of vomit around my neck, and I can even smell the honey-flavoured beer as it flows out my nose.

Finally, they crouch over my useless body and start robbing me: taking the watch off my wrist and the sunglasses from my shirt pocket. This doesn't make me happy, but at least it makes sense.

I begin to feel hands quickly running through the pockets of my jeans – four of them, one hand for each pocket. The loose bills and even some change is removed from my front pockets. Then my brand-new wallet, the one I bought yesterday at the Empire State Building and which has an impression of the landmark burned into the dark leather, is removed from my back pocket. Carter's condom, for some reason, they don't steal.

"Why?" Kendra asks.

Josh doesn't answer, so she asks again, but I know this isn't going to help, because Josh hasn't answered her all morning.

"Why? *Why* did you take him down there and then leave him alone? He's just a teenager, Josh. *What* were you thinking? A *bar*? He's four*teen*. What possessed you? What? Just tell me, please, *why*?"

I want to say, "He wasn't thinking," except the swelling under my eyes and in my lips is so bad that I can't speak very well. Instead, I just sit there and nod, which is about the only way I can communicate – not that there's much to communicate.

Last night, Josh found me lying in the street a few blocks from the bar. It turns out he had rushed out of the bathroom, looking for me after I ran away when I caught him doing coke, but he didn't know in which direction I had gone and so he ran all around the neighbourhood for almost an hour. By the time he found me, the blood on my face was already dry and I was sobering up enough to really feel the pain.

While those guys were beating me, it wasn't so bad because I was drunk and couldn't feel anything beyond the abstract tips of their boots pushing into what felt like a dead pile of clothes. The alcohol had made my whole body numb and I couldn't really tell what was happening, like when your foot falls asleep and you can't feel your toes or anything below the knee. But this morning, when I woke up, I could barely move. Every part of my body was sore and riddled with purple bruises. Kendra, when she felt my chest – which is covered with all sorts of bumps – thought I might have broken a rib. But Josh just laughed during all this and told me to "Walk it off". I could tell he thought I was being a baby, that whatever had happened to me was no big deal and that I was just complaining or over-acting in order to get attention. I knew that, in his eyes, I would always be seen as the harmless little brother, and that no matter how loudly I screamed in anger or yelled out of fright, he would always think I was just crying "Wolf".

Now, a few hours later, Josh and Kendra have propped me up on their couch. I'm as stiff as a mannequin. My bags are packed and ready to go, they're right by the door. My train leaves in an hour, but I don't know how I'm going to make it. How will I get in and out of a cab? It'll take a forklift just to get me on to the train. I'll need a human-sized shoehorn to fit into my seat. But I'd prefer that to staying here another second longer. Hell, I'd prefer sleeping in Central Park to staying in this apartment one moment more than I have to.

"Goddamnit, Josh, I need a reason for what you did. To make me understand, because as it is. . ." Kendra halts in mid-sentence, and I can tell from her passionate voice that the words are flowing out of her mouth quicker than she can form ideas. She's thinking off the top of her head, and what's pouring from her mind is the utter bafflement and disappointment in her husband's — my brother's — actions.

"Kendra, just shut up, OK? I'm really, *really* tired of hearing you yell at me. It's all you've done all morning." Josh doesn't even look at her, he keeps his eyes on the door, where my packed bags sit right next to the large Sunday edition of the *New York Times* I know he's dying to read. "Why don't you go make some waffles or something."

"You rotten bastard. I should leave right now and—"

"Yes, Kendra, leave. And go where?" Finally he raises his head and looks at her. "Would you go wherever you were last night?"

"I told you, Josh, I was out. With a *friend*. With Steph, for God's sake. Call Ben and ask him!"

"Yeah, right. That's bullshit, Kendra. Fucking bullshit!"

"I swear . . . Josh."

"Bullshit!"

I close my eyes for a few seconds while they continue to argue, and the sound without picture conjures up memories I haven't thought of in a long time – almost a lifetime: I'm young and my parents are still married. We live in Slater, Rhode Island, which is the little town in which I was born and where we lived until my parents got divorced and Josh went away to college. Unfortunately, this is what most of the memories of my parents' marriage are like: the fighting, the shouting, and me sitting between them, scared, wondering, hoping it wasn't my fault, praying that they weren't shouting at each other because of me. My brother's voice, in its raspy deepness, even sounds a little like my father's. Kendra's voice doesn't sound like my mom's, but every scared woman's voice is sort of sadly the same.

When I finally open my eyes, unable to take any

longer the visions appearing in my head, I look at my brother with blurry vision – blurry because there are tears in my eyes – and from this distance and through the saltwater, he even *looks* like our dad. I begin to fear that my brother's going to make all of the same mistakes as our father, starting with driving away a wife who really loves him.

"OK, Josh, are you through? Are you done accusing me? Because I don't think Perry needs to hear any more of your insane, paranoid ramblings. Do you, Perry?"

Suddenly I'm drawn into their shouting match, except, instead of answering, I just sort of shake my swollen head ambivalently back and forth. My response could be read as either "yes" or "no".

Whether it's for my sake or not, Josh decides to take a break and stops yelling. Instead, he gets up and crosses the room, switching the stereo on to a radio station playing jazz. The music calms me down, and after Kendra leaves the room and then comes back with a wet washcloth in her hand, which reminds Josh that it's his turn to do the laundry, everything almost seems normal again. I can't believe that just a few minutes ago these two seemed ready to kill each other.

"Jesus, Perry, what is your mother going to think?" Kendra asks as she raises the washcloth to my bruised forehead. She delicately swabs my face with the wet rag, mopping up the dried blood and soaking the purple scabs which have already grown over the cuts.

"Are you kidding?" Josh says from the hallway

where, after not being able to wait any longer, he's gone to retrieve the paper. "She'll baby him for a week. He'll do nothing but watch movies, eat pizza, and have ice-cream fed to him intravenously. It'll be the best time of his life."

This makes me laugh, but as my lips turn upward in a grin I re-split my lip and dark red blood – almost purple – dribbles on to Kendra's white washcloth. I look at Josh and think, *Best time of my life, my ass.*

"Here you go, Perry, try to drink this."

Kendra raises a glass of fresh orange juice to my lips, but each time I try to sip, the juice stings my cut lips so bad that I wince in pain. On her face is a hurt look, as if nothing's working out and it's all her fault. I want to tell her that it's all Josh's fault, but I figure she's smart enough to know that already.

Kendra gives up on the juice and picks up the wash-cloth again, dabbing with it here and there on my head. After a few minutes of watching us over the corner of his newspaper, Josh yells at her again.

"Will you just leave him alone?"

"What? Why?" Startled by his voice, Kendra pauses for a second. But then she shakes off his intimidation and continues. "I'm just trying to help."

"I know what you're *trying* to do, so stop it!"

"Josh, you're crazy."

"Kendra, I am *not* crazy. You're mothering him and he doesn't need that. He's already got a mother, remember? She's *my* mother, too."

"Yeah, well, I wonder what she did wrong that you turned out the way *you* are."

Instead of replying to this, Josh just sort of laughs under his breath.

In the ensuing silence, the room is filled with a thick tension, and the tension is making it feel much hotter than it already is. The sweat on my forehead mixes with the cool water Kendra keeps applying with the wet cloth, which runs down my face and on to my T-shirt.

"You feeling better, Perry?"

I just sort of nod.

"That's good. God, I'm *really* sorry this happened. Don't think worse of the city because of it. I've lived here for five years and nothing like this has ever happened to me. Really, don't hate New York."

I shake my head, trying to tell her that I don't hate New York.

"Just relax. Let the water cool you off. Here, let me get that."

Kendra grabs the washcloth from where it's dropped on to the hardwood floor. She reapplies it to my face, now using both of her hands as she massages my swollen head. I shut my eyes and, what she's doing feels so good, I almost fall asleep. Until, of course, Josh turns the page and sees us.

"What the hell are you trying to do, Kendra? Jack him off?"

"Josh, shut up. Just leave us alone."

"I'll leave you alone," he says.

But instead of leaving us alone, he gets up off the couch, throws the paper to the ground, and crosses the room, standing above Kendra and I. He slowly draws back his left arm, as if it were just a threat, but then he suddenly swings at Kendra, landing his open hand powerfully on the right side of her face. Unfortunately, I know exactly how she feels.

Kendra crumples to the ground, the wet washcloth falling out of her hand and on to my bare feet.

august

"I think your bruise looks cool."

Marina says this as she runs her right hand over the raised black and purple skin which sags underneath my left eye. Even though it hurts when she touches me, her fingers sending sparks of pain throughout my face, I let her touch anyway.

The rest of the bruises on my body have deflated in size and lessened in colour in the week and a half since I've been home, the various patches of dark purple turning yellowish or light green. Now I look almost normal except for the area around my eye, which is still discoloured and puffy. From the bridge of my nose through the left eyebrow and over the base of my right cheek looks like melted black cherry ice-cream. And Marina just can't take her eyes off of it.

"Wow, really? You think it looks *cool*?"

"Yeah," she says, sipping on a lemonade at the

counter of Gus's Diner, where I had the courage to meet Carter and her for lunch, after he had the nerve to invite me. I swear, Carter doesn't think that anything is a bad idea. "It's sort of rugged looking. Makes you look tough."

"*Tough?*" Carter says, almost choking on a French fry which the cook made him pay for in advance. "His face looks like a rotten piece of meat. How is *that* tough?"

Marina sort of squints at Carter's comment, but instead of turning to reply, she keeps her eyes trained on me. In the two months I've known her, she's never looked at me so seriously or for so long.

"When you left, Perry, you were a boy. Now, you're a *man*."

Even though I don't know exactly how true this is, I just let it sink in for a few seconds, not wanting to disturb the moment. Marina turns back to her untouched hamburger while Carter, with his elbows on the counter and a sour look on his face, finishes the food on his own plate. I just sip on my Sprite and savour the fact that a beautiful girl like Marina has just called me a Man. It's the first time I've ever been called one.

This is also the first I've seen of either of them since I've been home. In fact, today's really the first day I've been out of the house since I got back, except for the few times I went with Mom or Sis to the grocery store. I haven't been out because I was embarrassed about my face and by what happened. I knew that people would stare at me, wanting to know the rest of the story, wanting to know the background of my bruises and whether or not I deserved to look the way I do.

The first person I had to tell was my mother and, like Kendra predicted, she completely freaked out. On the train ride back to Walther, which seemed to last three times longer than the ride down to Manhattan, I came up with all sorts of stories I was going to tell her which would explain away my injuries: I fell down the steps at Grand Central Station, I was knocked over by a rollerblader in Central Park, an advertising executive on Madison Avenue pushed me into the path of an oncoming cab. These excuses would have worked for the bruises and scrapes on my hands and arms, and she might even have believed me for a minute or two – I can be real convincing when I have to be – but there was no getting around my black eye. I knew there would be nothing to explain away my face except the truth.

When I told her, she started to cry. First just a little, and then a lot. Finally she burst out into tears and pulled me into her chest, holding me so tight that I could feel her hot tears raining on to my head, drizzling over my hair and trickling down my scraped forehead. Her loud sobbing, there in the empty train station, scared me. She held on to me so tight that I didn't think she'd ever let me go, and I knew in her heart that she didn't want to, ever. She wanted to always hold me, keep me close to her, protecting me from every bad thing that was bound to happen the second she let go.

When she finally stopped crying, and dragged me

through the station (where all of the clerks were staring at us) and shoved me into the car, that's when she got mad. The terrified mother that I had just seen, who would have been played by Sally Field in the film, all of a sudden turned into The Terminator. Suddenly, Arnold Schwartzenegger was shouting at me, demanding answers. Who had done this to me? Where had it happened? Why? What had brought it on? Was there a reason? Was it, somehow, my fault?

When I told her that I didn't know why it had happened, but that I was pretty sure that the whole thing took place on Perry Street – spelled just like my name – she snapped at me, "Don't get cute!" Right after she said that I took a look at myself in the side-view mirror, and what I saw wasn't very cute at all. The whole left side of my face was ballooned up with a terrible amount of swelling, my lips were the size of two thick cigars, and under my chin were four cuts which refused to scab over because every time I tried to talk I broke the little cuts filled with clotted blood like undoing a zipper, which caused me to bleed all over again.

She continued like this for the whole drive home, yelling at me, making me feel worse than I already did. When we got back to Sis's, Mom called Josh to yell at him but he didn't pick up. Instead, there was just the machine that only had Kendra's voice on it, and this made my mom all embarrassed and she didn't even leave a message.

When Marina gets up to use the restroom, Carter slides over one space and sits next to me, occupying his sister's vacated stool.

"Sorry you had to hear that, old sport. Marina's always been a sucker for the Marlboro Man type. It's only been the last few years that she's stopped hanging around boxers. You wouldn't think you could unhook a bra wearing those gloves, but you can." Carter laughs for a second at his own joke, but then wipes the imaginary tears from his eyes and turns serious. "But I'll tell you what *really* makes you a man. Imbibing all of those libations."

"What? Speak English."

Carter rolls his eyes, as if he doesn't know why he continues to be friends with me. Then he lowers his voice and whispers, "Getting drunk, doofus. Now *that* was pretty cool."

"Carter, *that* was pretty stupid. That's what caused me to get beat up, being in that bar. You know, if anybody had found out I was drinking, I could have gotten into lots of trouble."

Suddenly Carter's face lights up and instantly I know I've said the wrong thing. The words "lots", "of", and "trouble" are still ringing in his head and I can see that, behind his eyes, he's making all sorts of plans.

I know I shouldn't have told Carter and Marina what happened, but I had to. With my face looking the way it does, it's an impossible secret to keep. Besides, even though all I did was act as two guys' punching bag, because of it I've gained Carter's respect and Marina's sudden interest.

By the time his sister comes back, Carter's been silent for five minutes and I've just been pushing a cold pair of fish sticks around my plate, hoping he'd say something to change the subject. But instead he's just been sitting there, looking devilish, planning something. And I'm smart enough to realize that whatever it is he's planning includes me.

"So, Carter, have you told Perry about next week?"

When Marina returns, she sits on the stool that Carter had been sitting on. She swings herself around, coming to a stop facing the rest of the diner instead of the plate that Carter has wiped clean. Crossing her legs, her black skirt is pushed up, exposing tanned thighs.

Just to get my eyes off those legs, I turn to Carter and ask, "Next week? What's next week?"

"Orientation," he says glumly.

"For Walther High," Marina adds, since Carter is obviously unhappy with the idea. "You know, you pick your classes, they assign you a locker, take your picture for your ID. You can sign up for baseball or football or to be a cheerleader. Stuff like that."

I've never gone to any kind of orientation at my other schools, but it sounds like a good idea. It'll give me a chance to check out Walther High before the first day of school, so I'll know what to expect.

My record for the first days of school is mixed at best; none of them have ever been entirely horrible, but they've never gone really well, either. The worst part about the first day of school, I think, is the anticipation. For weeks beforehand I have bad dreams about what it's going to be like. The nightmares range from the standard paranoia (like I'm going to leave my notebook at home or no one's going to like me), to the completely absurd (such as my mom dropping me off in front of the campus and I'm completely naked). I've had the nightmare about being naked for the past five years. It never fails.

Now that it's August, school is less than a month away and I can't believe it. I feel like all I did was blink and half the summer has passed me by. I would blink right now in order to get through the rest of the summer, except it hurts when I blink, so I just sit there, staring at Marina's legs.

"I can't believe we'll be at the same school, little brother."

"Yeah, well, just don't embarrass me."

"I should say the same thing to you."

"Yeah, right. *Me* embarrass *you*."

"Why should it be any different than what happened at Christmas?"

"Bring that up again, Marina, and I swear I'll. . ."

"You'll *what*? Huh? What?"

After a week spent with Josh and Kendra, I'm an expert at seeing when two people are going to get into a fight, and I can see that happening right now. To try and derail their argument, I say, "Hey, Marina, how come you don't go to a private school the way Carter does? I mean, *did*."

"Believe me, Perry, private school's not all it's cracked up to be. The girls are usually snotty, the food's always rotten, and Walther's where all my friends are. Besides, public school is co-ed. And the only reason Carter went to so many prep schools is because our parents wanted him out of the house."

Carter stops picking at the fries on Marina's plate and says, "It's true. The last one was all the way down in Pennsylvania. I think I came home maybe three times all year. They didn't even come to parents' weekend."

"Why not?"

"Oh, who knows? Or cares? I think they'd like to send me to Switzerland and never see me again, except they know I wouldn't go. I'd hijack the airplane and make it turn around and come right back. If they think they're punishing me by making me live at home and go to public school, well then I'll punish *them* by actually doing it."

"Seriously, Perry," Marina swings back towards the counter, the hem of her skirt dropping to below her knees. "My parents are pretty fed up with him. They're escaping to California for a vacation starting this weekend. I think they're staying in a spa or something. That's the only way to really cleanse yourself of a person like Carter: sit in mud for five days."

She starts laughing, but all of a sudden stops and checks her watch.

"Shit, Carter. We've got to get out of here. Paul's meeting me at the house at six, and it's already past five. Come on, let's go."

Carter warily nods his head, shoving the last few of her French fries into his mouth. I walk out with them, but decline their offer of a ride home, which I think Marina's grateful for since it would make her even more late than she already is. It's such a beautiful day, not too hot and with a cool breeze, so I'm looking forward to the walk home.

"See you next week, Perry!" Marina calls through her open window as she starts the engine. "And don't forget, I really love the bruise!"

Before Carter gets in the car, he takes me aside on the sidewalk and says, "So, you think getting drunk makes you a man?"

"No, Carter, that's what *you* think. And your sister loves the black eye. I swear, you Hannons have really got a screw loose."

"Yeah, well, we'll see who's *really* a man. OK? One of these days, I'll show you."

On Tuesday morning Marina and Carter pick me up for the orientation, not that either come to the door. Instead, Marina just honks three times, the horn of her black BMW short and high-pitched, sounding more like a whine than a warning.

When I crawl into the backseat I notice that both of them are dressed up, as if they were going to brunch at their country club and not to their high school gym to pick some classes. Marina's wearing a black cocktail dress and black sandals with large heels which are attached to her feet with skinny leather straps. On her face is so much white make-up and red lipstick that she looks like an actress from one of those Japanese plays I see every once in a while on Channel 13.

Carter is wearing a pair of khaki pants which are stiff with starch, a beige linen shirt with creases running down each arm, and brown penny loafers which look like they've just been polished. His hair is slicked back with a perfumy-smelling gel, and cologne rises off his body. He looks more like a model than a freshman.

As Marina pulls out of Sis's driveway, I look down at my own clothes: a pair of old blue shorts and a green polo shirt which is faded from years of wear. My shoes are old Treton tennis sneakers, marked with black streaks and the soles worn smooth. I'm not even wearing socks.

"Wow, you guys really look nice," I say.

Marina catches my eyes in her rear-view mirror.

"I told you they were going to take pictures, didn't I?"

"Yeah, but just for our IDs. That's not too big a deal, is it?"

"That all depends," Marina says, taking her eyes off of me and turning them back to the road. Maybe she's disappointed because my black eye has started to go away, along with the rest of my bruises. I actually look somewhat normal again, but to a girl like Marina there's nothing exciting about a guy who's normal.

She follows the main road through town, passing by the square with its green copper statue of Alec Walther, and then Gus's Diner and the library which has a banner over the arched entrance announcing the exhibition of original manuscripts by local authors.

Walther High is just a few blocks away from the main part of town, tucked behind a large patch of trees which give way to a cleared out area where a cluster of red-brick buildings sit beside a stadium which has an oval track set up with hurdles around the football field.

Marina guides her BMW quickly and expertly down a two-lane road behind the stadium to a half-filled parking lot where fifty or so kids are gathered around, sitting on the hoods of cars, talking and smoking and drinking what's probably beer from brown paper bags. Behind a chain-link fence which skirts the perimeter of the lot, there's a large white sign that says in big black letters STUDENT PARKING and underneath, next to a Camaro where two kids in the front seat are passing what I think is a joint back and forth, NO SMOKING.

"This lot is so trashy," Marina says as she pulls into a vacant space far away from any other cars. "I used to park in the faculty parking lot, but they kicked me out last year."

"How did they find out you were a student?"

As she slides her seat forward, allowing me to escape from the small backseat, she says, "It was easy for them to figure it out. There's no *way* a teacher could afford a BMW."

As we begin to walk away, she hits a button on her key-chain which causes the car's headlights to flash on and then off, along with a high-pitched electronic beep.

"So, sis, where is it they usually hold this shindig?"

"It's in the gym, you moron. You know that."

After Marina says this, she starts to walk quickly, putting distance between herself and Carter and I. I guess this is pretty much the way it's going to be at Walther High. After all, a junior can't be seen talking to two freshmen.

As we walk between a trio of large buildings which Carter points out are filled with classrooms, I notice how different this school is from the one I went to last year. In Tucson, everything was outdoors: lockers, drinking fountains, dozens of benches where you could eat your lunch. Even the classrooms were separate, spaced a few metres apart like tract houses, connected by sidewalks which were covered with tin awnings in case it rained.

I tell Carter all this, describing what my last school was like, but it just makes him laugh.

"Yeah, that's because you were in goddamn Arizona, old sport. In January, you were probably still walking around in shorts and a T-shirt."

"Well, yeah."

"But this is the *East* Coast. There's going to be snow, thunderstorms, hail, lots of rain. It's going to be ten degrees *below* zero. If you had to run from class to class, you'd freeze halfway. Kids would be lying everywhere, turning into icicles. *Dead.* How would that make the school board look, huh?"

What Carter says makes sense, and I guess I was stupid not to realize it on my own. From the few years that I can remember of my early childhood in Rhode Island, I've got scattered memories of picking up my brother in the winter from a high school made up of large brown buildings. To me, strapped into my car seat, they looked like apartments because of the dozens of windows, all of them lit up a bright yellow, as if inside families just like ours were having their dinner in front of the TV.

By the time we pass the library, Marina's already ditched us, and we figure out where the gym is by following a stream of kids headed in the same direction. Finally we come to a set of double doors above which is painted the Walther High mascot: a peacock with two wings raised in a fighting position, little fists poking out of the brilliant plumage.

Once inside, Carter and I are swept into a jumble of kids trying to figure out exactly where they need to go. Carter just stands there, waiting for me to take the initiative, so I shove my way to the front of the crowd where there's a directory taped to a blackboard. In the background, there's the constant low hum of hundreds of voices speaking at once.

"I think we need to be over there," I shout into Carter's ear.

He nods in a silent approval, and lets me lead the way. As we make our way through the sea of bodies, I look up and see on the scoreboard the score of the final basketball game of last season: Walther lost by twenty-eight points. With a peacock as a mascot, it's no wonder.

It turns out that the gym is divided into different sections for different grades: the seniors are all huddled near the back bleachers; the juniors are assigned to the rear entrance; while the sophomore class is meeting under one basketball hoop and the freshmen at the other.

I can see where a lot of the upperclassmen and women are treating the day like a mini-reunion, asking their former classmates how they've been spending their summer and what classes they intend to take in the upcoming year. The seniors all look especially cocky. On their faces is the sly assurance that soon they're going to rule the school.

Because the freshmen have yet to go through a year together at Walther High, there's less conversing and mixing in our part of the gym, but I can still see where clumps of students from the two junior highs are gathered together, trading gossip about their various alumni who are going to Patterson instead of Walther High. But in whatever direction I turn I see the various freshmen, all of whom look a little scared, clinging to one another like frail cells hoping to multiply. It's obvious that there's strength in numbers.

Intermixed with the clumps of casual acquaintances I

see a few groups of old friends, guys and girls who must have gone to school together since kindergarten. I look at them with jealousy because I've never had anything like that in my own life. The longest I've ever had a friend was maybe a few months, maybe even less. Even the relationships with my father and brother ended after just a few years, when Josh went to college and my mom divorced my dad and she and I moved several states away.

Some of the kids around me have lived in Walther their entire lives, while for as long as I can remember my mom and I have criss-crossed the country like tourists, visiting places for long stretches at a time but never really *living* anywhere. In fact, whenever someone asks me where I'm from, I never know what to say.

"Over there, Carter." I point to the corner of the basketball court. "That's where they're taking the pictures for the IDs."

Once again he nods, but this time he takes the lead, and I follow him.

Even though Carter's never attended school with anyone in the room, the kids swirling around us seem to know who he is. As we make our way to the line to have our photos taken for our identification cards, the crowd separates for us as we walk by, and I can see kids whisper to their friends and point as we approach. I guess that, as a Hannon, Carter's reputation precedes him. Everyone already knows who he is.

I wonder if they've all heard about what happened in

June at Gus's Diner. If so, then they know all about me, too. They've all heard that I (The New Kid in Town) was the one who was in with Carter on the whole thing. This makes me smile, to be thought of, if even for a second, as an accomplice, as someone faintly notorious. Maybe they're all looking at the remains of my black eye and, by the first day of school, I'll already have a reputation as a tough guy and be feared in the halls. Who knows, maybe even the sophomores will be afraid of me.

"Can you believe this pathetic set-up?" Carter says to me with a sneer as we approach the head of the line.

He points with his thumb to a small camera that's set up on a tripod in front of a stool and a dark blue backdrop.

"What did you expect, Carter?" I try to keep my voice down, although it's apparent that the girl in front of us and the guy standing behind me can easily hear our conversation. "Did you think they'd paint our portraits in oil?"

"Of course not, old sport, but *this*? I mean, he's not even using a flash! Do you know what that's going to do to my skin colouring? I'll look like I've got malaria!"

The girl in front of him enters the small area, reluctantly shows her shiny smile of teeth covered with braces, and then hops off the stool. Somewhere in there her picture was taken, but the photographer never said exactly when. This makes me groan, and I begin to think that Carter is right. These are all going to look like mugshots.

Now that it's his turn, Carter saunters up to the stool, turns it around twice, wipes it off with the back of his hand, and then gently sits down. He crosses his legs and then clasps his hands and places them on his knees, his long fingers interlocking like braided hair. He really does look striking, sort of like a painting you'd see in the biography of an important person which showed what the subject looked like when they were young.

"Hey, Mappelthorpe!" Carter calls out to the man behind the camera, who pretends not to hear. "Why don't you go back to taking photographs of big black guys with whips sticking out of their—"

But the end of his sentence is drowned out by the click-and-whir of the camera. Carter quickly hops off the stool, produces a ten dollar bill from his leather wallet, and gives it to the photographer.

"Here you are, my good man. Be sure to send me twelve wallet-sized. And keep the change."

This elicits a hearty laugh from the small crowd of kids who have gathered to watch the show Carter is putting on. Even though the photographer, a man with grey hair in his fifties, is obviously embarrassed, he takes the money and shoves it deep into his green polyester pants.

Carter steps out of the small area, allowing me to enter. I quickly sit down on the stool and face the camera, trying to sit up straight so that my large shoulders don't appear hunched over in the photo, which they sometimes do because my posture's so bad.

To the left of the camera, I can see Carter standing

behind the photographer. Most kids would make outrageous faces, trying to make me laugh, but Carter's got too much class for that.

"For God's sake, old sport," he calls out, "at least give the guy a small smile. *Some*thing to work with."

It's the second time he's called me "Old Sport" in front of the others and I wonder if the kids around us, who have been listening and watching, have taken note of this. In my dizzy head I suddenly have another fantasy. I dream that on the first day of school everyone will greet me by calling out in the halls, "Hey, Old Sport!" I've been going to this school for five minutes and already I have a nickname. Maybe none of this will be as bad as I thought.

"Next!" the photographer calls out, pulling me out of my daydream.

I get up off the stool and rejoin Carter, who suggests we find where the schedules are being handed out.

"Over there, I think."

"Lead the way."

I fight our way through the crowd to the middle of the basketball court, where two tables are set up, one with a sign that says A-L while the other has a sign that reads M-Z. Carter and I are about to fold into our separate lines when, through the crowd, I see a face that looks familiar. It's a girl wearing an orange summer dress with a brown leather backpack slung over a tanned shoulder. When she turns to hear something a friend is saying, I get a good look at her and suddenly my body feels like it's been electrocuted. I think my heart may have stopped, that all of the blood rushing throughout my body has suddenly frozen in place. I can't believe it but . . . there she is. *Donna.*

"Holy . . . Christ. . ." I sputter.

"What is it, old sport? You're turning all white. Well, whi*ter.*"

I can't even speak, so instead I raise my arm and point. He follows to where my finger leads to a face in the crowd.

"Oh," Carter says, "*her.*"

Donna is standing with two other girls, throwing her long hair back as she laughs at someone's joke. I can tell that, even though I can see her, she still hasn't spotted me. A few students pass by on their way to register for their electives, and for a second I lose Donna in the crowd. I begin to think it was just my imagination, that I've dreamt the whole thing, but then the crowd thins out and I see her bright face once again. I can't believe how beautiful she looks. My eyes break my heart.

"Well, go say something to her."

"What, *here*? Now?"

"Yes, *now*. In an hour everyone will be gone and you'll be the only one here."

"Jesus, Carter, I don't know."

"Aw, come on. Besides everything, what have you got to lose?"

"No, really. I can't. What would I say?"

"'Hello', for starters."

"No, Carter, I *can't*. My heart's racing a mile a minute and I think I'd collapse before I even made it to the free-throw line."

"Listen, if you don't say something to her *right* now, you're going to whine about it all day – and I'm not going to let that happen. Me having to listen to you, I mean."

I feel his hand on my shoulder, nudging me forward, and it's just the push I need to start to wade into the crowd of students. Suddenly I'm right behind Donna, even though she still doesn't see me. Standing there, I can smell her perfume and it makes me almost as drunk as I was back in New York.

"Hi," I say, getting her attention.

It's so loud in the gym that I can tell she hasn't recognized my voice, and that she's just turning around out of instinct, because it's what has been happening to her all day: turning around to say hi to a friend she hasn't seen for months.

When she finally sees me, she says flatly, "Oh, it's *you*."

"Listen, I'm sorry for the phonecalls. For everything, really. But I've got to talk to you."

She takes her eyes off me and looks over my shoulder. She sees Carter standing in the distance, his eyes on us, obviously trying to eavesdrop.

"So, I see you're still tethered to your little friend."

"No, Donna . . . it's not like that. If you'd just listen. . ."

The line she's standing in moves forward so she turns away from me and advances a space on the parquet floor.

"Please, Donna, won't you talk to me? Just for a few seconds?"

"Perry, I'm busy. Just . . . leave me alone."

A few sophomores start crowding around me, trying to get in the back of the line. Donna still won't turn around to look at me so I leave, heading back towards the freshman section of the gym. I bump into a couple of students and knock the notebook out of some girl's hand. "Hey!" she yells, but I just keep reeling backwards, numbly taking steps away from Donna.

Finally I bump into the padded gym wall. I turn around, away from the crowd, and lean against the smelly canvas covering. Carter appears by my side a few seconds later with a puzzled look on his face.

"How did it go?"

"Not good."

"So then, you won't be needing these prom tickets I just bought? They're selling them right over there." He lifts up two pieces of paper and points with them towards where the bleachers are folded like an accordion and bolted to the wall.

"Funny," I say, even though there's nothing funny about any of this.

In the past couple of weeks, I had managed to forget about Donna and what had happened between us and what I was beginning to feel for her. After what happened to me in Manhattan, I had plenty of other things to worry about.

Every once in a while I'd think of her, and want to call her on the phone to tell her what happened – like that morning at Josh's when Kendra made waffles – but I knew she wouldn't speak to me so I didn't even try. For the rest of July I sort of shoved Donna out of my mind, forcing myself not to think about her although, at times, I still did. I just couldn't help it.

I knew that the first day of school was approaching and that I'd probably run into her a couple of times during the year, but I guess I blocked all that out of my mind. I really hadn't considered it, or what I would do when it happened.

Coming here today, sitting in the backseat with Carter and Marina as they argued about what radio station to listen to, I really had no idea that Donna would be here. But she is, and even from this distance I can see how attractive she is. Her mouth opens and closes, but I can't hear what she's saying because I'm surrounded by stupid kids who don't care about what's going on inside of me. They're all concerned with themselves, with their own lives and problems, but I know that there's no way in the world any of them can be going through the same thing I am.

"Fuck it," I say, "I'm getting out of here."

I turn to go, but Carter stops me.

"You're just going to leave?"

"Yeah . . . I have to. . ."

"But what about your classes? Your schedule? You still don't even have a locker yet. And wait till you see the PE uniforms. Our school colours is a rainbow. You know, because of the peacock and all."

"Really, Carter, I couldn't give a shit."

To take my eyes off Donna's face, I look at Carter. He's biting his bottom lip, as if he's making a very large decision in his head.

"OK, then. If you're going, I'm going, too."

"What? But what about *your* classes? *Your* schedule?"

"Oh, screw that stuff, old sport. We'll pick them up on the first day of school. You think I'm going to leave you alone when you're like this? You're liable to stick a fork into a quart of Ben & Jerry's and eat it like a lollipop."

We walk around the perimeter of the gym, trying not to draw attention to the fact that we're blowing off the rest of the orientation. After getting lost near a field of bike racks, we emerge from behind the auto-shop building and find the road which leads to town. Even though we don't really discuss it, it's obvious we're going to walk back instead of waiting for Marina.

"Carter, thanks for leaving with me. You didn't have to, you know."

"Don't worry about it. The way I see it, you're still new to Walther and you probably wouldn't have found your way back. Besides, I figured I sort of owed you one. Now we're even. OK?"

I smile for the first time in days.

"Sure."

"Hey, listen, my parents are coming back Saturday, so why don't you come over Friday night? We'll just hang out and celebrate one of the last flings of the summer before we both have to go to this wretched place." He waves his hand towards Walther High, which is getting smaller and smaller the further we walk.

"Yeah, sure. That sounds cool."

"Just come over at eight. Call me beforehand and I'll give you directions."

"OK."

As we continue to walk, mostly in silence, I look over at Carter and am amazed to see him, as well dressed as he is, casually walking in the dirt by the side of the road.

I still can't believe what he did for me back there. I might have lost it, or made a real fool out of myself, but Carter helped me keep it together. Behaviour like that makes me think that maybe I was wrong about him, that maybe Carter's not the complete jerk I thought he was. I mean, it takes a lot of effort for someone to be *all* bad.

It makes me wonder, *At what point do you really count someone as out? When is a mind* really *made up?* I thought I'd made my decision about Carter, but maybe I was wrong.

As I walk to Carter's house on Friday night, I begin to notice that for every home I pass the average income of the family who lives there rises by maybe twenty or thirty thousand dollars a year. It's incredible, but with every step I take towards the east end of town, away from where I live, the homes get more and more expensive. With every block, Walther gets nicer and nicer.

Sis's neighbourhood is OK, but you can tell it's lower middle class. You can tell the kinds of people who live inside the modest homes: small families, hard workers, newlyweds who just bought their first home and couldn't afford anything better. You can even tell what kind of jobs people have. On Sis's block, it's a safe bet that most of the men work with their hands: plumbers, carpenters, etc.; while the women are mostly secretaries or assistants.

But the closer I get to Carter's home, the houses multiply in size. They must have six or seven bedrooms and a dozen in all, once you count the various dens and studies and libraries and dining-rooms. Even the garages expand to hold not just one or two but even three cars, and some are so big that through glass holes in the front I can see small boats locked inside. Some of the garages alone are as big as Sis's whole house. Suddenly I feel like I'm way out of my league.

Whatever kinds of jobs the people on this block have, I know they're not plumbers or carpenters. In fact, I can't imagine these people ever get their hands dirty. They're probably lawyers, or doctors, or maybe they're bankers and traders, like all of those men and women in the dark suits who commute daily to the southern tip of Manhattan (where Wall Street is).

All my life, whenever I've seen houses this big, my first impulse was to believe that the people inside them were dishonest. I used to think that anyone who could afford a home like that was a liar or a cheat, an embezzler at best and a drug dealer at worst. I used to think this because I just couldn't fathom somebody earning so much money honestly, just by going to college and getting a job, because that's what most people do but most people don't ever get to own a house like this. Like, my mother is one of the most honest people I know, and we've always had run-down houses that were a notch above a mobile home (and I even lived in one of those for a while), so if someone like her can't make that kind of money, working as hard as she does, then I don't know who could.

By the time I get to Carter's house, it's completely dark out. Last month the sun was still shining past eight o'clock, and the days were so long I used to pray for them to end, but now, halfway into August, the weather's turning cooler and the days get shorter and shorter. On some nights – and tonight is one of those nights – when there's a cool breeze that makes you try and remember in what box you stored all your winter clothes, you can feel autumn waking up from its long sleep. You can tell that, in a few weeks, the leaves will fall off the trees and cold weather will begin again.

After walking the fifty steps that lead from the sidewalk to Carter's front door, which is actually two doors – each a dark brown wood with stained-glass inlay – I press a glowing button which activates a set of chimes somewhere in the house.

"Good evening, old sport, glad you could make it," Carter says as he swings open one of the doors, the light from behind him making him appear as just a silhouette.

I'm startled for a few seconds because I can't believe that he's the one who answered the door. I thought for sure the Hannons would have a maid or maybe even a butler.

"Normally I don't do this, answer the door, I mean, but Carmelita took the night off. Her daughter's giving birth or something like that."

"Wow," I say, entering the house. "She's having a baby?"

"Or maybe it's just a regular operation, I don't know. It was some dumb excuse like that. All I can remember is that it was an emergency and there was a hospital involved in there somewhere."

When Carter closes the door, the loud sound sends an echo throughout the cavernous house. In front of us a carpeted staircase with an ornate balustrade leads to the first floor, while large sets of double doors are on our right and left. Carter's house feels like the set of a gameshow, with all of those doors and unexpected treasures hidden behind each one.

"I suppose you want the tour," he says, sort of snidely.

It's obvious that he doesn't want to show me around, so I don't even ask.

"No, don't worry about it." I say this as casual as

possible, trying to sound as if I've been in homes larger than this hundreds of times. "Where's Marina?"

"Out with that guy, Paul. Probably won't be back until late. If at all."

While he leads me through a maze of hallways, I think about Marina sleeping with Paul and I'm stung with a foolish jealousy.

As we wind our way throughout the house, I look into all of the rooms we pass. Each one is bigger than the entire ground floor of Sis's house. First there's a dining-room with a table that must be five metres long; then there's a kitchen with two refrigerators and a stove on a large island in the middle of the room; after that is a library with leather couches and chairs, filled floor to ceiling with books; next to the library is a bathroom with brass fixtures, a shower, bathtub and even a bidet.

Finally we come to a den which is about the size of Sis's living-room and kitchen combined. Carter sits down on a large couch opposite a huge entertainment centre housing a wide-screen TV, stereo and VCR. The floor is littered with both a Nintendo and a Play Station, and in the corner cartridges are stacked in heaping piles.

"You going to come in, or what?"

Carter looks up at me from his reclined position on the couch. He's waving me into the room, but for some reason I don't enter, I just stand there clutching one of the double doors.

Suddenly I feel very out of place. I wish I were

outside on the sidewalk, running home and watching as the houses get cheaper and cheaper.

"Oh, yeah, sorry," I clumsily say, pushing myself over the threshold and into the den. I sit down on the couch but it's so large that, even though Carter's on the same couch, I can't see his face. There are too many cushions between us. Instead of looking at him, I watch the TV where Carter's flipping through so many channels so quickly that the screen looks like a strobe light.

"So, uh, what were you watching?"

"Ah," he says disgustedly, "damn satellite dish is acting up again."

"You have a . . . satellite dish?"

"Sure," he replies in a cocky tone of voice which seems to say, *Doesn't everybody?*

While he tries to find something that will hold his interest for at least a few seconds, I notice that situated upon the surface of a wooden side-table are half a dozen liquor bottles. Behind the bottles is a small bucket filled with ice, and next to that are two glasses.

"What's all that stuff for?" I ask, pointing to the six bottles.

"Oh," Carter says, suddenly interested, "that's for us."

He jumps off the couch and walks to the table. His back is turned to me, but I hear the *clink-clink* of ice-cubes being dropped into a glass, and then the *glug-glug* of liquor leaving the bottle. When he turns to me, just as I suspected, there's a glass in each hand.

"What the hell is this?"

"Why, it's vodka, old sport."

He hands me one of the glasses, but instead of taking a sip I just stare down at the ice-cubes swimming in alcohol. Carter sits back down on the couch, takes a deep drag of his drink, and then starts changing the channels, one every second. He acts as if nothing strange has happened.

After a few minutes of just holding the drink, letting the cold sweat from my glass drip on to the couch, Carter turns to me.

"You going to drink that, or what?"

Instead of giving him the Yes or No answer he requested, I say, "Jesus, Carter, *vodka*? Why?"

"Well, I know it's not beer, like what you had down in jolly old Manhattan, but the elder Hannons have never been terribly fond of fermented hops."

"Which means what, exactly?"

"My dad didn't have any beer in the fridge. Besides, beer's so un*sophis*ticated. You'll be in college one day — most likely — and then you can have all the beer you want. Until then . . . why not live a little?"

Carter raises his glass for a toast, but I just sit there.

"Come on, old sport, what's the big deal? You're letting me down. Frankly, I was pretty impressed when you came back from New York City and told me you'd had a few."

By "a few" I guess he means drinks. I told him everything about my New York trip, about all the museums and the famous landmarks, but I guess all Carter is interested in is the stuff he's not supposed to be interested in. If you tell Carter "No", he'll spend the rest of his life turning that word into "Yes".

"You know, school starts soon. Just a couple more weeks now. And I would hate to see you become ostracized so soon into your high school career."

"'Ostracized'? What does that mean?"

"It means you'll be left out. *That*'s what it means. Not only won't Donna talk to you, but no one else will, either. After all, why would someone want to hang around a scared puss who won't have a drink now and again?"

"Carter, you wouldn't," I say, even though I knew he would.

I should go, just get the hell out of here, leaving Carter and his screwed-up friendship behind. But I don't. I stay because, whether he talks bad about me at Walther High or not, it's going to be hard enough starting all over again at a new school. Besides him, I don't know anybody. Sure, I'd probably meet people after a while – in school it's always sort of inevitable – but I don't want to have to wait that long. Besides, I hate all of those awkward steps you've got to go through before you make friends.

For too many years I've sat alone in cafeterias, or killed time in the library before class, or been the last one picked for baseball and football teams. For most of my life I haven't belonged, been the odd kid out, and I don't think I can stand going through that again, especially in high school when it's really going to count.

"OK, Carter," I say, raising the vodka in my hand. With my full glass I tap his, the sound of glass on glass rising over the noise of a commercial in the background. For some reason, I feel like I've just made a deal with the devil. Well, maybe not the devil, but I definitely made a deal with Carter. I figure that's close enough.

"Good, good. Now, to refill my own. You'd better hurry or I'm going to lap you."

I take a quick sip, letting the liquid sit on my tongue until it starts to burn my mouth so that I have to swallow. It goes down easier than I expected, except right afterwards my mouth is filled with the vapour of what tastes like gasoline. I inhale madly for fresh air which, of course, makes Carter laugh.

"Maybe straight vodka's *not* your drink. Hang on a second, I'll go get some orange juice. That'll cut the taste a little."

After Carter leaves the room, I stare into my glass which is now only half-full. I figure now I could slip out and he wouldn't be able to stop me, or I could at least pour the rest of my drink into the ice-cubes. But I don't do either of those things. I just sit there and finish my vodka in another quick, flammable gulp. I figure that if I'm going to do this, I'd better do it right. And the quicker I get drunk, the less there will be to remember in the morning.

"I feel like a flat tyre."

Now it's after one o'clock in the morning and Carter

won't shut up about this, about how *punctured* and *empty* he feels inside, which is all a metaphor, I guess, for being unhappy. I want to tell him to shut up and inform him that no one's really happy, but he just won't give me the chance. He won't shut up about how much he feels like a flat tyre. We've been drinking steadily all night, and so far I must've heard him say this about twenty million times.

"A flat . . . I mean . . . you know, I feel like a . . . like one of those round thingies . . . on a *carrrrr* . . . a flat . . . tie-ear-rah."

Carter barely finishes his favourite sentence before falling off the couch and on to the floor. He breaks into hysterical giggles and begins rolling around, curling himself into a little ball. For someone who feels so flat, he's able to make his body awfully round.

"Lishen, Carter, thass great." After all of these hours, and all of those drinks, my own speech, when I dare to talk, is slow and slurred. "But itsh late and I've gotsch to go."

"No, no, pleashe. I'm show flat, no . . . don't *leave* me. . ."

"Carter, yesh. I've gotsch to. Itsh *late*."

Suddenly he springs to life, jumps off the floor and lands wobbily on his feet.

"Well, then, I'd bedder drive you."

"No, you'd bedder not. You're *way* too drunk. I'm jush going to walk."

I turn to leave, but instead I trip over a book on the

floor and fall into the hallway, face down on the hard-wood floor. For some reason, we both think this is the funniest thing in the world. When we finally stop laughing, Carter helps me up and leads me through the winding maze of hallways to a white door in the kitchen.

"The garage," he says, punctuating his words with a burp.

Off a row of metal hooks placed below a spice rack, he takes a set of keys. Flapping against the brown leather strap I can see a metal key chain which says RANGE ROVER.

"No, Carter . . . thish ish a . . . *bad* idea. . ."

He opens the door and we enter the garage which holds, unbelievably, four cars: Marina's BMW, a silver Mercedes convertible, a white Saab station wagon and, at the far end, a hunter green Range Rover. The Range Rover is huge, with a ski rack on top and a bike rack fastened on the back. Above the fenders are whips of dried mud, which makes me figure that this car is Mr Hannon's answer to middle age.

"Come on, we'll take the four-by-four. Maybe we'll do shum off-roading."

"I think you'd bedder keep that thing *on* the road as mush as poshible."

Once again, this is the funniest thing we've ever heard, and by the time we've stopped laughing, we're in the car and Carter's got the engine started.

I'm not so drunk that I don't put my seatbelt on,

forcing Carter to do the same. He has trouble getting his attached (something he's done a hundred times, now that he's drunk, has become very difficult). Now that we're both strapped in, Carter puts the car in reverse and begins revving the engine. Seconds after he releases the clutch, there's a loud crash and Carter and I are thrown into our seats. The entire room is shaken, dust falling from the rafters and on to the windshield.

"Oh, yeah," he says plainly, "the door."

He inches the car forward, trying to unhook the rear of the car from the mangled garage door. Giving the engine a quick jolt, the Range Rover lunges forward, suddenly free from the door, and bashes into one of his dad's tool benches. I look behind us and can see that the bike rack is now stuck in the bent door.

Carter grabs the garage door opener from the armrest between us and keeps clicking it over and over, as if it were the remote control to the TV and he were looking for something worth watching.

"Come on, damnit."

As one of the sections of the giant garage door begins to open, I can see in the moonlight that Carter's eyes are half-closed while his mouth is open, drooling a long string of translucent spit on to his burgundy polo shirt. This is, I think, not a good sign.

"Damn . . . stupid . . . door. . ."

Because of the bump in the door caused from Carter's earlier mistake, the garage door won't open all the way. He tries to back out the car anyway, but when he does, the ski rack on top of the Range Rover gets caught and is torn off.

"Purr-fect," Carter says, backing down the driveway and into the street. As he pulls off into the night, I look into the open garage and can see smoke rising from his father's tool bench.

"Uh, Carter? I think you'd . . . I mean we'd . . . I think I'd bedder. . ."

But instead of listening, he steps on the gas pedal which causes us to fly down the road with such speed that once again I'm thrown back in my seat. I feel like I'm on a rollercoaster, except that in the back of my mind I know that this is real.

After taking a couple of turns, overcorrecting each time so that the Range Rover wobbles from side to side before Carter straightens it out, he asks, "Now, where do you live again?"

I look around but it's so dark and I'm so drunk that nothing looks familiar. Besides, Carter's driving so fast that nothing flashing before us has a chance to register in my alcohol-soaked brain. The windshield looks like a TV screen with Carter constantly changing channels.

After a while of heading down various dead-end streets and even the long road which leads to Patterson, Carter and I end up circling the square in downtown Walther. Because it's so late – it must be two by now – all of the stores are closed, even the movie theatre and diner. Each of the shop windows is dark, but some have an eerie glow because of a light left on somewhere inside. As we blaze past Gus's Diner, Carter driving on the wrong side of the road, I can see that all of the chairs are sitting upside down on the tables.

"Carter, I think you'd bedder . . . shlow . . . down. . ."

He's piloting the Range Rover around the square at an extremely high speed, which seems to increase every time we pass around, as if we're a rubber band being wound tighter and tighter. Suddenly I begin to feel nauseous, and think I'm going to throw up. I look over at Carter, to beg him to pull over, and when I do I see that he's practically asleep. His eyes are closed almost all the way; he must be steering purely out of instinct.

"Carter, come on, *stop*. . ."

He doesn't respond, and by now I'm feeling really sick. The motion of the car is causing all of the liquor in my stomach to make waves which lap all the way up my throat. I burp and a thin stream of vomit dribbles down and then over my lips.

"Please, man, pull over. . ."

Again he doesn't respond, so finally I shout out to him, "Carter!"

As if yanked out of a deep sleep, his eyes pop open and his arms rigidly take control of the wheel. Instead of going straight, he pulls into a sharp turn which launches us over the kerb and on to the sidewalk, heading into the square in front of the library.

The Range Rover instantly sideswipes a drinking fountain, destroying the small stone foundation and causing the faucet to spurt water like a miniature geyser.

Then we run over a few benches, but none of them can withstand the power and force of the large car, which crushes each of them as if they were made out of Popsicle sticks.

"Carter, no, watch out for the. . ."

Illuminated before us and approaching fast is the statue of Alec Walther. Even though it's pitch black outside, the large copper figure is lit up by four lamps, one of which we narrowly miss. I can tell that Carter also sees the statue, but he's too scared to react. His arms gripping the wheel remain locked in place. I reach over to try and grab the wheel, but it's too late.

The Range Rover collides with the base of the statue with a tremendous amount of force, collapsing the front of the vehicle instantly. Carter and I are thrown forward, but are then held back by our seatbelts and also two airbags which explode in our faces. The force of the impact raises the back of the Range Rover high into the air, and when it lands all of the side windows shatter, raining down beads of glass.

Still in a daze, I look up and can see that the statue of Alec Walther is teetering back and forth. Even though the statue's pedestal is barely scratched from the incident, the impact of the crash has knocked the loose screws right out of the base of the statue.

All of a sudden, in what looks to me like slow motion, the large figure falls off its pedestal, diving right for the ground. Carter, still conscious, giggles and says quietly, "Timber."

When the statue lands on the concrete, Alec's green head breaks off cleanly at the neck. The head then rolls unevenly down the sidewalk, away from the scene of our accident, towards the sound of sirens which are becoming louder and louder. Police or paramedics or both will be here soon.

"Shit!" Carter yells, as if for the first time figuring out what's happening. His eyes open wide and his face is filled with terror. It's the first time I've ever seen him scared.

As the sound of sirens becomes even more intense (and from the jumble of noises I can tell there are lots of cars headed this way), Carter fumbles with the seatbelt, wrenching himself free. I try to do the same thing except I can't feel anything in one of my arms. I look down and see I'm covered with blood, but I'm not sure exactly from where the blood is coming.

"Oh, shit, man. Shit," Carter's mumbling. "I've got to get out of here."

When he sees that I'm not moving, he reaches across my body and unhooks my seatbelt. He then pulls me out of the seat, dragging me over the armrest. He backs his way out, shakily standing on the concrete, and then pulls me into the driver's seat. I wait for him to pull me out, too, but he doesn't. He just leaves me there, behind the wheel which is bent into a taco shape.

"I'm sorry, old sport, but I can't. . ."

His voice is temporarily drowned out as two police cars and a fire engine turn the corner and enter the square. The library steps in the distance are lit up by the red and blue lights of the police cars, the flickering colours looking like fireworks.

"I can't let them find me behind the wheel. My dad will pay for everything, don't worry."

He turns to run away and I try desperately to follow him, but I still can't move. My legs feel numb and the fingers on my right hand are tingly and in my left hand I can't feel a thing. Looking down, I see the dull white of one of my bones sticking out of my long-sleeve shirt which is now stained dark purple from blood.

Raising my head, and dizzy from pain and fear, I see Carter limping away, into the shadows. He calls out, "Don't worry!" just as a dark blue police car pulls up beside the remains of the Hannons' Range Rover.

I hear a number of car doors open and close, and then I pass out.

I haven't been in a hospital since the first time I was anywhere, which means the day I was born, but I don't remember that day too well. Actually, I remember it about as well as I remember last night, which is almost not at all.

Actually, that's not true. Certain things keep coming back to me, a detail here and an image there. Little bits of information become clear, each coming into focus at a different time. I can't make out what the entire thing looks like, but here and there I see dots and patches of clarity. I figure the police will fill in the rest.

One of the things I can remember, and truly see clearly, is the image of Carter's face when the car jumped the kerb and headed into the square. His eyes were finally wide open, his lips were separated as if to yell but there was no time to scream, and his arms, paralyzed with fear, were stretched out straight as if they were two boards nailed to the wheel.

The rest of last night is just flashes of light and images, horrible crashing sounds and the smell of smoke from burning rubber and pouring gasoline. I can even remember the face of Alec Walther in the Range Rover's headlights as we sped closer and closer and then, after the crash, when the writer's head rolled down the sidewalk.

It turns out that my left arm had been broken pretty badly (in two places), but other than that my injuries were just the usual scrapes and bruises. It turns out my numbness and inability to move were just symptoms of the shock I was going into (instead of the beginning of a lifetime of not being able to feel anything below a certain point in the body: the neck or the waist or wherever).

This morning I drift out of sleep due to the deep voice of some doctor who keeps telling me over and over how lucky I am to be alive. I look down at my arm, which is in a cast, and then bring my good hand to my face, to find it bumpy and sore with bruises, the bruises that had just healed called back for a repeat performance. I don't feel very lucky.

"It was the air bag that saved you. Even though you were wearing a seatbelt, the force of the impact would have pushed the dashboard right through your head." As the doctor speaks, he doesn't even look at me, he just keeps glancing at my chart and fingering the dressing of my wounds. I get the feeling that he's really talking to himself, enjoying the sound of his own voice. His bed-side manners are bad. "Consider yourself lucky that you were driving a Range Rover. If it had just been an old Toyota or something, you wouldn't be here right now. You're very, *very* lucky."

Yes, I think, *if you're going to have jackass friends, make sure their parents drive expensive cars.*

"Wait a second, *I* was driving? But I was just. . ."

I try to explain but the doctor just waves his hand at me, as if to suggest that all of my energy should go towards my recuperation and not a futile denying of what he knows is the truth. After all, the police must have told him that I was the only one in the car, the only body found at the scene. *This boy here, he's the one who done it.* It might even be written on that chart he keeps looking at. Near my name, at the top, might be the one word which says it all: GUILTY.

For the rest of the morning I'm visited by a parade of doctors and policemen, all of them asking difficult questions. The doctors want to know where it hurts ("Everywhere," I tell them), while the various law enforcement officials want to know what happened ("What do *you* think?" I answer).

The facts of the case are apparent and easy to figure out. I was found at the scene of an accident behind the wheel of a car registered to Mr Patrick Hannon. Since I'm only fourteen, was drunk at the time, and did a lot of damage, a whole slew of laws must have been broken. In my daze, I begin to wonder just how far Carter is going to let me take the blame. For all I know, he could have hobbled off to a pay phone and reported the car stolen.

After breakfast (which I don't even touch), the police begin to leave me alone. I guess it's because I'm so young and no one was really hurt (except me), so they stop treating me like I'm a murderer. They know that I'm not going anywhere, so for a while all of the questions stop.

Finally, at around ten, my mother is allowed to see me. One of the nurses said she's been here all night, nervously pacing in the waiting-room downstairs. I guess she was there when I was brought in, and was holding my hand all during the setting of my arm and for the dozen or so stitches above my right eye, but I don't remember any of that because I was still pretty drunk and also in shock. I do remember a few things, like the strange sensation of feeling a threaded needle puncture my anaesthetized skin, and then the slathering of the wet plaster on my shattered arm. I also remember an awful lot of crying, a seemingly never-ending stream of tears coming from somewhere. I guess that was Mom.

"Hello, baby," she says as she slowly walks into the room, as if she's frightened by what she might find. Her eyes look like blisters, round and red and puffy, and I doubt that she can cry any more. I doubt that there's anything left. My mother has been wrung out, and there's no more water in the cloth.

"Mom, I'm so . . . sorry."

Now I start to cry, except it hurts when I do, the stitches still tight in my forehead and my cheeks covered with fresh scabs.

She reaches down and hugs me the best she can, her small arms barely fitting around my large white cast. Feeling her close to me makes me cry even harder, even though it stings when I do, and when she finally pulls away there's a dark wet spot from my tears on the shoulder of her blue sweatshirt.

"Mom, it was dumbest thing I've ever done but it wasn't me . . . it was Carter. I *wasn't* driving . . . I swear to you. . ."

After sitting down on the bed Mom sniffles twice, then raises her hand to silence me, which is just what the doctor did earlier. Today, no one wants to hear me speak.

"I know, son, I know. I figured as much. That spoiled little bastard. But that still doesn't excuse *your* part in all of this. Where do you get off? Drinking alcohol. You're fourteen years old, for God's sake!"

I'm tempted to tell her about Josh, about what really happened in New York, but that seems like ancient history now.

"I know, it was dumb. Completely, absolutely stupid.

And I'm sorry. You can ground me for the rest of my life. I probably deserve it."

She looks towards the hallway, and then says, "I think there's a couple of cops in this town who may take care of that for you."

"You mean, I'm going to be arrested?"

"Oh, Perry, don't worry about it. I'm sure that was just to scare me. Once they found out that I had insurance, they weren't so interested in sending you to the slammer. After all, you're just a kid."

For the first time in my life, it's a joy to be called "Just a kid".

"Listen, baby, you feel better, I've got to stop by the office and make some calls. I want this whole mess straightened out so we can get you back to Sis's. All right?"

She gets off the bed, but leans over and gives me another hug.

"OK, Mom. But come back soon. Please? This place makes me nervous."

"Why?"

"I don't know, it just does. It smells funny. It smells like that stuff you make me use to clean the bathroom."

My mom laughs and says, "Ammonia."

"Yeah," this makes me laugh, but that hurts, too. "That's the stuff."

"OK, I'll come back as soon as I can."

As she leaves, I can hear her heels striking the shiny white floors. All the way down they make noise, *clack-clack-clack*, until the sound grows fainter and fainter and then she's gone.

Bored, I turn to the window. The view out of my fourth-floor room looks over the parking lot (which was built around a helicopter pad, which really is just a square patch of concrete about the size of a basketball court with an H in the centre in bright red paint).

For an hour or so I just watch the traffic in the parking lot, all of the cars coming in and going out. There's a steady stream of fathers and sons and mothers and daughters on their way to visit sick grandparents who do nothing but sleep, cry and forget things; or else the family is here to check out the newest grandchild who does nothing but sleep, cry, and has the world in front of them to learn. Seeing all of these happy families, striding arm in arm (sometimes a kid is on the dad's shoulders), makes me wonder how many beds in the hospital are taken up by punks like me, dumb idiots who have injured themselves in some stupid, selfish way. They ought to have a ward just for us, where the other patients are wheeled through every half-hour so they can makes fun of us, spit on us, and painfully pull out the tubes stuck in our noses.

The door to my room opens with a creak, and I turn quickly from the window, hoping to see my mom or maybe Sis or Bob, but who I see instead is Carter. He sheepishly enters, looking sort of embarrassed, but also sort of bored. Standing next to him is a tall man with grey hair wearing a pink linen shirt and white pants. He looks like a golfer. No, he looks like a lawyer *trying* to look like a golfer.

"Good afternoon, old sport. How are you feeling?"

"What the hell do you care?" Before Carter has a chance to answer, I add, "Who's this, your legal counsel? Are you going to sue me because I bled on your upholstery?"

"Uh, Perry, this is my dad."

The man smiles and extends his hand, which I painfully lean forward to shake. When I sit back, I can feel that my palm is oily and stinks of cologne. Carter's father is lean and handsome, with skin tanned a deep bronze. His hair is silver, but on him it looks good, making him appear wise and distinguished.

"My son explained to me what happened," Mr Hannon says, his voice deep and authoritative. If Carter's scared of him, I can see why. "And I just want you to know that there's nothing to worry about."

"What in the hell are you talking about? There's been cops in and out of here all morning. My arm's fractured, my face is all cut up, and I'm pretty sure they're going to arrest me. There's *plenty* to worry about."

"First of all, I guarantee you that the police will take no formal action against you. Whatever charges they were considering filing have been dropped."

"Dropped? But how? Carter knocked the head off Walther's literary hero and wrecked a Range Rover in the middle of the town square. Doesn't anybody care about that?"

"Let's just say that I have many a friend in the Walther Police Department, and that last night's activities are going to be reported as nothing more than a simple accident."

Because Mr Hannon didn't flinch when I mentioned Carter's name, I figure that he really does know what happened last night. He must know that Carter was behind the wheel, that we were both drunk, and that his son fled the scene leaving me to take the blame. I guess Carter, for the first time in his life, told the truth. But his dad doesn't seem to care, he just wants to settle this whole ugly matter as quickly and as quietly as possible. After all, skeletons are made to be hid in the closet, not hung on a clothes-line.

"And, of course," his father continues, "whatever bills there are, they will be quickly taken care of. I promise that you will never be in need of expert medical care."

"Yeah, great, thanks."

"In return, I ask only that you treat the events of last night with a respectful degree of discretion."

There's silence for a moment as my bruised brain figures out what Carter's dad is really saying: he wants me to lie. If anyone asks me what happened, I'm supposed to say that I did it. That this whole mess was *my* fault.

"Come on, old sport. I'm counting on you."

I look up to discover that it's Mr Hannon who has called me "old sport", not Carter.

"Sure, I'll be discreet. I'll say whatever you want me to say. Just . . . just get the fuck out of my room, OK?"

Without another word they turn around and begin to leave, Mr Hannon leading the way. While he's waiting for his dad to exit, I examine Carter to see if he's got any cuts or bruises. There's not a scratch on him. There never will be.

"OK, Perry . . . give it a try."

I'm standing in the living-room, Sis and Mom are behind me and Bob's in front holding a contraption he constructed over the weekend. It's sort of a cross between a desk and a stand, like one of those fold-out trays which people use to eat their dinners on in front of the TV, but this is a support for my broken arm. Bob told me he made it out of scraps he had lying around the workshop behind his house (which is an old converted storage shed). On the flat open space of the stand there's another piece of wood about thirty centimetres wide rising up from the surface by ten or twelve centimetres; this is so I can rest my arm while eating or turning pages or – and I think this is really why he made me the thing – for writing in the journal he gave me. "Don't want you falling behind in recording everything, do we, Perry?" he said when he dragged in his invention an hour ago. I haven't got the heart to tell him the book is still blank.

"Well, come on, Perry," my mother calls out, "we don't have all day."

Finally I drag myself to the couch and sit down, placing the stand in front of me. Bob puts the remote control for the TV beside the raised platform, and when I put my arm on the block of wood I realize the rubber buttons on the remote control are at the perfect level so that my fingers can punch up any channel I want. Magazines or books will slide perfectly under this little ledge, and it'll make eating easier, too, by supporting my heavy arm's weight when I'm eating a sandwich or my Fruit Loops in the morning. First my room and now this; Bob's quite a genius.

"It's perfect," I say, looking up and glancing at Mom and Sis but staring at Bob for a few seconds. I want him to know how much this means to me. When he notices that I'm staring at him, Bob becomes self-conscious and embarrassed, and looks away. His face, like a boy's, floods with colour and he blushes bashfully. Once again I'm struck by the question of why he doesn't have any kids of his own, or why he and Sis won't get married. "Really, Bob, thanks."

"Aw, it was a cinch," he says modestly, even though the half dozen Band-Aids on his hands and arms show it wasn't so simple after all. "And down here, there's a place for magazines and *TV Guides* or snacks or whatever."

The four of us, even Bob, tilt our heads to the bottom of his invention, where our eight eyes notice a little shelf he's wedged in between the four legs of the stand. He runs across the room, grabs an issue of Sis's *People* magazine, and sets it on the little shelf. It fits perfectly. Just as I'm about to ask myself the question, *Is there anything that Bob can't do?*, the answer floats to the surface of my mind: *Yes, he can't have a kid of his own and he can't get Sis to marry him.*

Since the police never filed any charges and because there was nothing really wrong with me – that is, nothing that required a stay in the hospital – my mother was allowed to bring me home the day after the accident. I've been here for nearly a week now and it's been like this most of the time: Sis, Mom and Bob spending their evenings standing over me, being nice, wanting to know if there's anything they can do or get for me.

But the first night I was home, Bob didn't come by and Mom and Sis kept to themselves, spending hours sitting at the table in the kitchen drinking coffee and whispering about something back and forth. It didn't take much of an effort to figure out that it was me that they were talking about. For a whole night I was their topic of conversation, about how worried they were over what was going to happen to me, and what they could do about it. Both of them, from what I overheard, were very worried. In fact, I'm not sure who was worried more although because my mom had given birth to me, she certainly had the emotional home-court advantage.

For the first few days I just propped myself up in the living-room with a few pillows to support my heavy cast, and set up around me an array of chocolate bars, bags of potato chips and cans of Sprite. I could tell that the rest of my summer – all two weeks of it – would probably be spent this way: doing nothing but watching TV. And that's what I did, for the most part.

On a couple of nights Mom and I had a few nice talks, evenings during which we sat around and watched TV and remembered times when we were a little happier than we were right now, not that we've ever been completely happy. It seems that there's always been something – or somebody – in our way, and it was weird to realize that, this time, that something was me. It wasn't one of my Mom's divorces that was creating the tension in the house; it was because of something I had done. I began to feel guilty, thinking that everything in Walther had been going fine except for me making all the wrong friends and crashing into statues.

I tried to make things better by cleaning up after myself around the house and doing the dishes and taking out the trash which was always piled high in the kitchen from all of our pizza boxes and buckets of fried chicken, but with my arm in a cast and my body still sore from the accident, I wasn't much of a help. There were all sorts of things I couldn't do, and help was one of them.

Two days after Bob gave me my little stand (the "crutch-hutch", I've named it), there's a light knock on the door. I can tell that it's not the mailman or someone peddling religious pamphlets, because the touch on the door is dainty and almost not even there; it's as if whoever is outside doesn't want me to hear.

In the past week I'd been ignoring anyone who came

to the door, not needing Girl Scout cookies or to get reacquainted with Christ, but this morning I'm so bored that I'll buy or listen to anything. If nothing else, I need the sun I'll get just by opening the door because after a week and a half spent on the couch, sitting in the dark living-room, I've been getting paler and paler.

I get off the couch and shuffle into the hallway, and instead of looking through the peephole to see who it is, I just throw open the door. Standing on the other side is Donna.

"Hi," she says in a nervous exhalation of held breath.

"Hi," I reply, not knowing what to say next.

For a few seconds there's nothing but silence.

"Look, Perry, I just wanted to stop by and say how sorry I am about how I acted at the orientation. It was stupid."

Thankfully, Donna takes the initiative and begins to speak. If she hadn't, I probably would have just stood there and stared at her all day. She's wearing a pair of khaki shorts and a white T-shirt that says HUNTER in green letters, which is I guess a college she wants to go to. Slung over one shoulder is a brown leather backpack, the one she had at the orientation. Her hair is swept back into a pony-tail, just like it was on the first day I saw her back in June, that day at the diner.

"Maybe I didn't handle it too well — or even what happened at Gus's — and for that . . . I apologize."

"No, Donna, it's my fault. I was the jerk."

"I know you were, but . . . I probably should have let you explain, and I didn't. I just avoided you and wouldn't listen at the orientation and never returned your calls. And for that I'm sorry. Really."

Since we're both awkwardly standing there, she on the doorstep and me inside the house, leaning against a coat rack, I decide to ask her inside. I know that the living-room is filled with countless Ruffles and Doritos bags, and maybe a dozen empty cans of Sprite – my crutch-hutch looking like the counter in a cheap deli – but I figure that I'm past the point of being able to impress Donna. After everything that's happened, there's nothing left to hide.

"Listen, why don't you come in?"

"Oh," she says, surprised. "I mean, yeah, sure."

Even though I step aside, she bumps up against my cast as she enters the house.

"Sorry. Does it hurt?"

"Nah, just itches, mostly."

I point the way to the living-room, where she sits down on the couch, tossing her backpack at her feet. I sit across from her on a wooden chair, the kind that are in the kitchen. I brought this one in so I could put my feet up while I watch TV because Sis, for some reason, doesn't have a coffee table. Since she's dating a wood-shop teacher you'd think she'd have coffee tables everywhere, but she doesn't. I push the crutch-hutch into a corner and Donna's too polite to ask what in hell it is.

"You *sure* your arm doesn't hurt? Don't feel the need to act tough just for me."

"No, really, I swear. Everything else hurts, trust me, but not the arm."

This makes her laugh a little and, even though it's dark in the room, I think she's blushing.

"So, uh, have you seen Carter lately?"

Donna says this with hesitation in her voice, as if it's a question she knows she should ask but doesn't necessarily want to.

"No. I mean, he and his *daddy* visited me in the hospital the day after the accident, just to let me know that their money was going to take care of everything. Since then he's called me a couple of times — maybe five or six — but I never talk to him. I don't want to. Not after all the shit he's pulled this summer."

"I know. I mean, Perry, you could have been killed."

Donna touches my arm for emphasis.

I know I shouldn't say what I'm about to say, but I don't care: I just say it.

"The only thing bad about being killed is that if I had been, I wouldn't be sitting here with you right now."

"That's sweet," she says, even though I suspect she thinks what I said is a bit corny. "Uh, listen, I should go."

"Go? But you just got here. I want to hear about what you've been up to, how you spent your summer, and about what happened with you and the diner and all of that. We've got a lot of catching up to do, don't we?"

Donna sort of smiles – the smile I remember.

"Sure, Perry, and I'll tell you all about that stuff, but I just can't do it right now. I've got to go, *really*. It's not just an excuse. I've got to be somewhere. Honest."

When she sees the worried look on my face, she adds, "School starts next week. We can talk then. OK?"

Since there's nothing I can do, and because I don't know any of the words that will make her stay, I dumbly nod my head.

"OK, then," she says, getting off the couch.

I get up, too, and walk to the front door, holding it open for her. Halfway down the steps she stops and turns around.

"I almost forgot."

"Forgot what?"

"I got you something, because I thought you'd be bedridden after the accident. Well, *couch*ridden."

She takes the backpack from her shoulder and places it on the ground, unlatching the flap on top and digging her hands inside. From in between a notebook and her purse she pulls out a brown bag.

"Here."

"What's this?"

"Look inside and find out, silly."

I reach into the bag and quickly pull out a small hardback book called *The Collected Tales of Alec Walther*. The cover is an old-fashioned portrait of the author sitting at a desk covered with scrolls; behind him a long quill pen sticks out of an inkwell.

"I thought you might want to get to know the man you beheaded."

"Hey, Carter did that. I was just along for the ride."

"Not according to the *Tri-Countier*."

"Really?"

"It was just a small little story, don't worry about it. Anyway, I've got to go. See you next week?"

"Yeah," I tuck the book under my good arm and wave as she descends the rest of the steps. "See you next week."

I watch as Donna crosses the street, heading west at the corner. For a half-hour I stand there on the porch and replay the memory in my head, like rewinding a movie: Donna smiling and turning away, saying "See you next week." Donna smiling and turning away, saying "See you next week." Donna smiling and turning away. . .

That night I can't wait for Mom to come home so I can tell her the news. I can't wait to tell her that Donna came over earlier in the day and that I think she might actually give me another chance with her. I also want to let her know that I can do without Carter and his friendship, and that I'm just going to ignore him and make a few real friends at Walther High.

I was so anxious to tell my mother all this that I began to get a stomach ache, as if all of my important news was winding itself around my heart and lungs, making it hard for me to breathe. I felt that if I didn't tell somebody soon about what I was feeling, I just might die.

But when Mom finally walks in the door, at a few minutes before eight o'clock, there's a strange look on her face – a look I've seen before. I can tell that she has news of her own.

"Perry," she says, "I think you'd better sit down."

"What, Mom? What is it?"

Instead of answering, she leads me into the living-room where I can still smell Donna's perfume even though that was all hours ago.

My mother slowly sits down on the couch, her gold coat still on and her briefcase in her hand.

"What's up?"

"Remember how I told you that my office has another branch in New York? Upstate?"

"Yeah, yeah, you told me. So?"

"Well, today I had to drive up there to help out on some paperwork because they were short staffed. You know how August is, everyone wants to take a vacation before the summer's over. Anyway, when I was up there, sorting through the files of unsold properties, I came across a little house. A beautiful house . . . a *perfect* house. And affordable, too. Two bedrooms, nice kitchen, located on a quiet little street. Back yard and every-thing. Picket fence – like in a movie. I guess it's been on the market for three years but there's never been even a nibble, although I don't know why because the place is just terrific."

She finally stops talking, almost out of breath from her speech.

"Yeah, so? It's a nice house, big deal." But then it hits me: she's a realtor. "Oh, you mean you *sold* the house? Oh, Mom, that's great. Congratulations! Wow, then we *both* had a great day."

"Well, yes, Perry, I sold the house. But not in the way that you think."

"What do you mean?"

"I mean, I sold the house, yes. But I sold it to . . . *me*."

"To *you*? I don't get it."

"I mean, I've been saving ever since we got here, and have kept my eyes open for a place just for us, so we could get out of Sis's hair, and so you could have your own room, a *real* room. And I finally did it, Perry. I paid the down payment earlier today. It's ours."

I get up and walk across the room, like I'm going to leave the house, except that there's no other place I can go. I turn back around and see Mom sitting on the couch, her briefcase in her hands and a nervous smile on her face. I can tell that what she's saying means the world to her, but it's the last thing in the world I want to hear.

"But Mom, *where*? Where is this place?"

"Batavia. It's a quaint little town upstate, about an hour away. Oh, Perry, wait till you see it. You're going to love it. It's so beautiful, it really is. It's what I've always dreamed about. Our own place, *finally*."

"Yeah, but . . . *when*? When do we move?"

The shine in my mother's eyes suddenly disappears, just like turning off a lamp.

"Saturday," she whispers.

"Saturday? *This* Saturday? Three *days* from now, Saturday?"

"Yes."

Suddenly all sorts of images and problems begin racing through my head; familiar images and problems.

"But how am I going to get to school if we live an hour away? Will I take a bus? I mean, are you going to drive me every day?"

"No, son, don't be ridiculous. You won't be going to Walther High. Batavia's got its own high school, of course. You'll be going . . . there. And me, I'll be working out of the Batavia office. I've already received approval for my transfer."

She laughs a little, as if I should have figured this out myself, which I should have. I guess I just didn't want to believe it.

"What? *Another* school? *Another* new town? You've got to be kidding me!" I collapse on to the brown recliner which sticks halfway into the hallway. My cast knocks against my bruised hipbone, but I don't notice the pain. "Jesus Christ, Mom, not *again*. How many times are you going to pull the rug out from under me, huh? How many?"

"I swear to you, honey, this will be the last time."

"That's what you said before, on the way here, to Walther. I remember your exact words, 'This will be the last time, honey.' You even called me *honey* last time, too."

"Well, I'm sorry, Perry, but this time really *is* the last time."

"How can I believe that? How can I believe *anything* any more? I mean, I finally like it here. Donna came over today and. . . This year she's going to . . . I mean, we just might. . ."

Since there's no use in arguing, because her mind's made up, I get off the chair and storm into my room, slamming the door behind me.

"Really, son, I swear!" I hear my mom call out from the living-room. "This *really* is the last time!"

The voice through my door is muffled, making her sound far away. I close my eyes, and when I do there's nothing but darkness and it seems like my mom is in a cave. I think to myself, *Good. The farther away, the better.*

"Perry, *please*. Open the door."

Instead of doing what she says, I lay down on my bed. I grab a pillow and put it over my face, hoping to drown out her high-pitched pleas which she's continuing to shove under the door.

"Perry, do you think I *like* this? Did you think I *liked* dragging us all the way across the country and then having to live with my sister all summer? In the past ten years I've gone to everyone in my family for a handout, but now I've got a chance to end all that. We'll have our *own* house. Finally, Perry."

"Yeah, in Batavia."

But because I say this in a low voice, and through the pillow, my mom really doesn't hear me.

"What?" she calls out, thinking what I've said is important even though I was just being a smart-ass. "What did you say, honey? What was that?"

After a few minutes of gently calling out my name, my mother starts to get pissed off. Instead of tapping on the door, now she's pounding.

"Goddamnit!" she yells. "You come out of there this instant! Quit pouting, you little selfish shit, and get out here!"

Provoked, I jump off the bed, run to the door and swing it open. I'm standing face to face with her. Just as I'm about to answer (although I've got no idea of what I'm going to say), something in the look on her face silences me. Something in her eyes doesn't even make me bother.

She's looking at me like I'm a brat, like this is me being a jerk just for the fun of it, and that the last ten minutes – me telling her how I feel, about what Donna and even this shitty little town have come to mean to me over the past three months – has just been a variation of the temper tantrums I used to throw when I was three or four and didn't get my way. I might as well be making chocolate pies out of mud or peeing in a cup and calling it lemonade for as much as she's listening to what I'm trying to say. My mother is completely misunderstanding me, and I don't know what to do about it. I never have.

"Fine, Mom," I finally say. I say this because there's nothing else to say. At least, there's nothing else she wants to hear. If I had all the right answers, I'd spill them, but I don't. All I have to give her is what I know. So instead of what's right, I say, " OK, I'll go."

Today is the first of September. We're moving tomorrow and in two days I'll be a freshman at Batavia High. The summer is finally over.

Looking back on the past three months, I can see that mistakes were made – plenty of them. In fact, for a while it seemed that making a mistake was the only thing I could do right.

It's funny, but I think that maybe my mom saw all this coming because she kept the boxes we used to move back in May. Last night she dragged me into the garage and made me get down from the rafters all of these thick pieces of cardboard, which she expertly unfolded and turned back into sturdy cubes. They were the same boxes we had bought from the U-Haul place back in Arizona. They weren't even dusty. It's like the boxes were waiting for us, and knew it wouldn't be long.

PERRY'S THINGS. There were four boxes that said

that, and four boxes was again all I needed to pack my stuff because I really didn't buy anything new this summer. Except for the blank book that Bob gave me, and the Alec Walther book from Donna, everything else is just the same old stuff.

From the empty shelf I pick up the book Bob gave me and open it slowly, the virginal spine making a cracking noise when I do. I flip through the pages, beginning at the end, discovering that all of them are still blank. I never did get around to writing anything.

I'm just about to toss the journal into a box of T-shirts, when I see a few faint scratches of black ink just inside the cover. It's Donna's phone number. I rip out that page, crumple it up, and throw it away in the garbage can beneath the desk.

When I called her yesterday, to tell her I was moving, she sounded honestly disappointed, as if she had really considered giving me some sort of chance at earning her heart in the years to come at Walther High. Of course, there's no way to know whether or not she was being sincere or just telling a boy moving away what he wanted to hear. Maybe she was telling the truth; maybe she wasn't. Maybe I'm just being cynical about it all now to make myself feel better.

After we finished the conversation, I still couldn't figure it out – whether or not Donna was being sincere – and when she told me that she would be getting her driver's license soon, and that maybe she could come upstate and see me some time, well, by then I had almost stopped listening. I had forced myself not to care. I knew that Donna would never follow where I went, and that there was no way I could take the train every five minutes down to Walther to see her. Whatever we had between us – which was, I had come to realize, not much – was over for good.

The night before we move to Batavia, Josh and Kendra drive up to Sis's in a rented car to help us celebrate our last night in Walther. This seems a little strange to me, that we've been in New York all summer but they hadn't bothered to make the short trip; not until now, that is, because tomorrow the trip's going to be lengthened by an hour and I guess Josh would rather drive from Manhattan to Walther instead of from Manhattan to Batavia, which is what he's going to have to do the next time he comes to visit, which I figure won't be until Christmas.

Beyond the excuse about helping us say goodbye to Walther, the visit seems like a nice chance to let my mom and Kendra meet for the first time. Once she was done packing, my mom started running all over. She'd start in the kitchen by peering into all of the pots and pans, checking on dinner, and then she'd weave her way throughout the entire house, repositioning cushions on the couch or else the chairs at the table in the dining-room, where we're finally going to eat for the first time since moving here. She's been a wreck all day, first from the packing and now from the anticipation of meeting Kendra.

As they pull up, at a little past seven o'clock, I look through the curtain in the living-room and see Josh behind the wheel, Kendra sitting beside him with her long blonde hair up. They get out of the car, meeting at the tip of the hood, where they join hands and walk up Sis's short driveway to the front door.

"Per-*ree*," my brother says, acting as if it's been ages and not just a few weeks since he last saw me. I guess he still feels bad about my trip; what happened to me and what I witnessed between him and his wife. I give him a long hug and then move on to greeting Kendra. She's wearing a nice light blue summer dress which, because of the rapidly approaching fall, she'll soon be putting away with the rest of her summer clothes. She also gives me a hug, although she doesn't quite know how to manoeuvre around my cast.

"Oh, Perry," she says, looking first into my eyes and then at all of the little scabs on my face left over from the crash. Beginning to laugh, she says, "You just can't stay out of trouble, can you?"

Mom is standing in the middle of the hallway, waiting for the three of us to finish our greeting so she can finally meet her daughter-in-law, something which every mother probably looks forward to even if some are later disappointed with the results. Without a word Kendra crosses the short hallway and envelops my mother in a hug. When they separate, minutes later, both of them have tears in their eyes. *Women*, I can't help but think.

Sis appears and introduces herself and Kendra says

how much the two sisters look alike, even though I've never really noticed much of a resemblance. The three women, chatting amiably, go into the kitchen to check on dinner, which leaves Josh and I alone in the living-room.

"Shit, kid, it's true," he says, pointing at my cast which, over the past couple of weeks, has turned from bone-white to a slightly cream colour, fading over time and from its brief appearances in the sun. "How're you holding up?"

"OK, I guess." A few days ago I had my whole life bottled up inside me and I was sure that when I next talked to Josh it would all come pouring out in an unstoppable burst. I felt like I had so much to tell him, about this summer, about myself, but now that he's standing here all of that has evaporated like steam out of my head and I just want to look at him and enjoy the fact that he's really here. Everything that happened in the past three months no longer seems important. It is what's going to happen that counts.

A few minutes later Mom calls us to dinner, and the five of us sit around the table, enjoying the meal she slaved over for more than half the day. Throughout the dinner Kendra and Josh play the happy couple, fielding the numerous questions asked by Mom and Sis, and in each of their polite answers I can find no trace of the anger or confusion which I experienced last month in Manhattan. Their behaviour leads me to believe that either they're just acting happy for the sake of my mom, or else they've really worked out the differences between them. Unable to choose between these two choices, I figure that Josh and Kendra probably haven't solved any big problems, but instead have talked themselves into the belief that they're happy. In any event, I'm glad to see they're at least giving it a chance, and that they're still together.

After dinner I show Kendra and Josh around the house, and both of them think my room is pretty cool.

"Hell, a studio apartment this size, in the East Village," my brother says, "would cost a grand a month."

"Not to mention the broker's fee," Kendra says, laughing.

While Mom and Josh sit on the couch catching up on all the news of our various extended families, and Sis is in the kitchen doing the dishes, Kendra says she's hot and needs air. I suggest she go out to the porch, and to keep her company, I volunteer to go with her.

"It's nice being out here, Perry."

"Where, Walther?"

"Well, not Walther, exactly. But the country. Normally we manage to get away at least once during the summer. To the Hamptons or Berkshires or somewhere for a weekend, but this summer we were both too busy. Not to mention broke. Do you know," she says, turning to face me; when she does, the light from the porch on the house next door frames her face in soft light, "this is the first time we've been out of the city all year?"

There's no way I could have possibly known this, but still I shake my head and open my eyes wide. My mouth says, "Wow," even though, looking at her, I'm thinking of other things.

"It's funny," she says, sort of swaying so that every couple of seconds her body touches mine, which causes me to shiver even though it's warm outside, "but you can't see stars in Manhattan. There are too many lights, too many buildings."

I'd noticed that when I was there, that the night sky – even at three or four a.m. – was coloured a deep sort of purple rather than black, almost as if there were a sheet of canvas stretched from one side of the city to the other, and everyone beneath was just staring up at the underside of some kind of tent. It made me feel awfully small not to be able to see that far out, to stars and other universes and galaxies and beyond. It made New York feel like a sort of cage, probably the way my brother feels about his marriage to this beautiful woman standing beside me. I turn and look at Kendra, who's still staring up at the sky and moving back and forth, as if she's reacting to music coming from somewhere.

Looking at her, she seems like half a dozen granted wishes. But then I think that maybe she's not perfect: probably, she's not. My brother seems to love her, and yet I know that, at times, he also hates her. To me she's nothing but answers, but to Josh she's just a bunch of annoying questions. It makes me believe that not only are there two sides to every story, but there are two sides – if not more – to every life.

I turn to her and, for some reason, put my good arm around the slender trunk of her body and pull her into me. Before she knows what's happened (hell, even I barely know what I'm doing), I press my lips on to hers. She's rigid for a moment, and I'm betting she's going to slap me or scream or something, but slowly she sort of softens and her arms pull me even closer into her rather than push away. Her lips feel amazing even though I don't have much to compare her to (just Donna and a couple of other quick kisses in closets), but what Kendra's doing feels a million miles away from those other experiences.

"Perry, stop." She finally pushes me away, untangling her body from mine. "You're cute, but . . . really, you should know better. . ."

As if she were talking to me through the jetwash of a giant airplane, I only hear one or two words in the jumbled static of her voice, all my concentration currently being siphoned to parts of my body other than my ears: all I hear her say is "Perry" and "cute" and "better".

She takes a step on the porch, and then looks at me with a smile that seems to say that what just happened between us was not wrong, but just ill timed. Not that she'll ever kiss me like that next week or next year or ever again, but that *someone* will. That everything, even though I'm moving yet again, is not horrible or completely lost or even permanently stained. I used to say that I come from a broken home, but I don't think that's necessarily true any more. I come from a home that used to be broken, but now it's on its way to becoming healed.

"Perry, I . . . I'm going inside."

Kendra turns, opens the screen door and then enters Sis's house. A second later I can hear my mother and brother's voices rise upon the reappearance of his wife and her daughter in-law. Kendra enters their conversation but she's not so loud that I can make out the words of what's being said; instead her voice creates a sort of buzzing background noise to the silence of the black night. Looking up, I can see nothing but stars, and each one feels like a future.

One day you may find yourself on a porch like this with a girl like that, in a town like Walther – where I by chance landed for the summer – and if you do I hope your story has a kiss in it like mine, or maybe one even better (if that could possibly exist). Or you may find yourself with an even more attractive person on the porch of a house ten times better than Sis's – and what happens to you may make what happened to me look like very small news. Or you may not even find yourself at all, in which case I guess I'd say: *keep looking*. Because it's definitely worth it.

About the author

Jeff Gomez is the author of two previous novels, *Our Noise* and *Geniuses of Crack*. He was born and raised in Southern California, and currently lives in Manhattan, where he is working on a new book. Visit his website at: www.dontcallhome.com